TWO-BOY WEEKEND

"Jessica, please don't hang up on me." Christopher's voice was strained and pleading.

She swallowed, near tears. "Why don't you leave me *alone*?"

"Because I love you, Jessica. Don't you realize that? Your boyfriend can't love you the way I do. And if he knows about us . . ."

An alarm went off in Jessica's head. "What do you mean, if he knows? I haven't told him, and I'm not going to. Now just leave me alone!"

Christopher laughed. It was a disturbing, menacing sound.

"You wouldn't—" Jessica choked.

She heard the dial tone. He had hung up on her.

"This is crazy," Jessica whispered.

In her head, the word "crazy" seemed to echo. What if Christopher *was* insane?

Suddenly Jessica was afraid. She slammed the receiver down, then stared at the phone in horror.

Bantam Books in the Sweet Valley High Series
Ask your bookseller for the books you have missed

SWEET VALLEY HIGH

TWO-BOY WEEKEND

Written by
Kate William

Created by
FRANCINE PASCAL

BANTAM BOOKS
TORONTO · NEW YORK · LONDON · SYDNEY · AUCKLAND

RL 6, IL age 12 and up

TWO-BOY WEEKEND
A Bantam Book / April 1989

Sweet Valley High is a registered trademark of Francine Pascal.

Conceived by Francine Pascal

Produced by Daniel Weiss Associates, Inc.,
27 West 20th Street, New York, NY 10011

Cover art by James Mathewuse

ISBN 0-553-27856-8

Published simultaneously in the United States and Canada

Bantam Books are published by Bantam Books, a division of Bantam Doubleday
Dell Publishing Group, Inc. Its trademark, consisting of the words "Bantam
Books" and the portrayal of a rooster, is Registered in U.S. Patent and Trademark
Office and in other countries. Marca Registrada. Bantam Books, 666 Fifth Avenue,
New York, New York 10103.

PRINTED IN THE UNITED STATES OF AMERICA

O   0 9 8 7 6 5 4 3 2 1

TWO-BOY WEEKEND

One

"That was such an amazing tennis match. I'll never be that good." Jessica Wakefield sighed and propped her right elbow up on the open window of the Fiat Spider she and her twin sister, Elizabeth, shared.

Elizabeth, in the driver's seat, concentrated on the morning traffic as they headed for Sweet Valley High. Jessica shot her sister a look. "That's your cue, Liz."

"Huh?" Smiling mischievously, Elizabeth turned innocent blue-green eyes on Jessica. "Oh. Was I supposed to say, 'What are you talking about, Jess? You're a great tennis player'?"

Jessica smirked. "Something like that."

"Sorry," Elizabeth replied with a giggle. "What are you talking about, Jess? You're a great tennis player."

"Gee, thanks."

Elizabeth giggled again and added, "You *are* a good player, but you have to admit, you're not exactly in Kristin Thompson's league."

With a casual shrug, Jessica crossed her long legs in front of her and shifted in the convertible's bucket seat. "I could be, you know."

"Right, Jess," Elizabeth said knowingly. "Sure."

She couldn't resist smiling at her twin. Jessica always had enough confidence for two, Elizabeth reflected. And seeing their classmate Kristin win another regional junior tennis championship over the weekend had spurred her enthusiasm for tennis all over again.

But except for cheerleading—she was co-captain of the squad—Jessica's enthusiasms were usually very brief. She flitted from one hobby to another, one new favorite occupation to the next, with breathtaking speed and nonchalance. That was her style. It used to be her style with boys, too, until lately. At one time Jessica had prided herself on dating a different boy every week, but some weeks earlier she had truly fallen in love for the first time. Since then, she and A. J. Morgan had been spending most of

2

their free time together. In that respect, Jessica had been acting a lot more like her twin.

Elizabeth, four minutes older than impetuous Jessica, was always steady and thoughtful, mature and responsible. She prided herself on having one steady boyfriend. Reading, playing the recorder, and writing were some of her favorite pastimes, although she was also very active in school activities and could always be counted on to organize or head a committee. She spent long hours working on *The Oracle*, the school newspaper. She also liked having heartfelt talks with her best friend, Enid Rollins, or her boyfriend, Jeffrey French. All things considered, her personality and Jessica's were completely different.

On the outside, however, the two sisters were like carbon copies. Silky blond hair, blue-green eyes, perfect size-six figures, and classic American good looks made the Wakefield twins prime examples of the California girl. Each girl even had a dimple in her left cheek. If they were dressed alike, it took a sharp eye to notice that Elizabeth always wore a wristwatch and Jessica never did. For some people it was the only way to tell them apart!

"Well, anyway, I've got so much other stuff to do, I can't be great at everything," Jessica concluded cheerfully. She shot Elizabeth a sunny smile. "There's only so much of me to go around."

Elizabeth's eyes twinkled with amusement. "You're right, Jess—there's *so* much of you."

Jessica wrinkled her nose and poked her twin in the ribs. "Haven't heard any complaints lately," she went on, obviously referring to her boyfriend. She switched the subject as her thoughts turned to A.J. "I sure hope A.J. wins that essay contest. He's supposed to find out today."

"Keep your fingers crossed," Elizabeth said. "He's got some heavy competition." Normally, Elizabeth would have entered an essay contest, but she had been so busy with a Big Sister program that she and Enid had started that she had decided not to enter.

Two weeks earlier, the annual essay competition held by Sweet Valley's Samaritans' Club had been announced. A group of professional men and women, the Samaritans sponsored community events and promoted civic improvements. Every year the club organized the Citizens' Day Ball. During the ball, held at the Sweet Valley Country Club, there was an awards ceremony for all the people who had in some way contributed to the community. The official king or queen of the ball was always the high-school student who won the essay contest.

"A.J. will win," Jessica announced complacently. "He's such a good writer. I'm sure his essay will be the best."

"What was it on?" Elizabeth asked as she signaled to turn into the Sweet Valley High drive. "I know they were all supposed to be about Sweet Valley in the year 2000, but that's pretty broad." She looked at her twin. Jessica was looking very sheepish. "You *did* read it, didn't you?"

"Well, I was *going* to . . ."

Elizabeth rolled her eyes. "You're lucky he puts up with you, you know that?" she teased, turning the car into the parking lot.

"Luck has nothing to do with it," Jessica replied in a lofty tone. She gave her sister a wink and hopped out of the car. "As Ms. Dalton always says in French, I've got that certain *je ne sais quoi*."

Elizabeth opened her door and swung her book bag over her arm. "Right, Jess. See you in chemistry."

Jessica sent her a serene smile. "*Au revoir*, Liz."

By the time Jessica got to her locker, she had already been waylaid by three of her friends, and was relieved to see A.J. still waiting for her, as usual.

"Hi, there," he drawled in his Georgia accent. He and his family had moved to Sweet Valley from Atlanta recently when his father had been posted to the nearby army base.

"Hi yourself." Jessica tipped her head back as he bent his head to kiss her hello. "What's up?"

A.J. tossed his thick red hair out of his eyes. "Nothing much," he began hesitantly. "Actually, remember how I told you my grandparents in Dallas are having their fiftieth anniversary?"

"Uh-huh." Jessica started to dial her locker combination. "So?"

"Well, all the relatives got their act together, and we're having a big party for them—on Friday." He looked pained. "And we're going."

Jessica raised her eyebrows. Having A.J. gone on Friday and Saturday night sounded utterly dismal. "To *Dallas*?"

"Yes, ma'am. And we're leaving Wednesday—"

"*Wednesday?*" Jessica's voice rose. "What are you doing, walking to Texas?"

A.J. shifted his books from one hand to the other and shook his head. "I knew you'd have an attack." He sighed. "My folks figure if we're going, we might as well have a good long visit

6

with the family. So we're leaving late Wednesday afternoon and coming back Sunday night.''

Jessica let out a groan. "I can't believe you're doing this to me! What am I supposed to do all that time? Sit around writing love letters?"

"That'd be nice," A.J. said with a smile. He pulled her to him and grinned down at her while she pouted. "Come on, Jess. It's just a few days."

She tried to look severe, even though being in his arms still gave her goose bumps. "I guess I'll just have to miss that party Ken Matthews is having."

"Why can't you go by yourself?" A.J. asked. "It's not like you have to lock yourself up in your room the whole time I'm gone."

"Forget it. I can't go to that party without you—it wouldn't look right," Jessica insisted. She ignored the fact that before she'd met A.J. she had never let not having a date stop her from going anywhere. The prospect of spending a weekend without him made the entire week ahead seem like a marathon of depression. The problem with having a steady boyfriend, she reflected sourly, meant everyone expected them as a couple. Going anywhere by herself now seemed like settling for a consolation prize.

Already she was beginning to feel neglected and abandoned.

A.J. was looking at her with an understanding expression in his brown eyes, and Jessica felt herself blush. It was incredible how well he knew her, even after such a short time. He always seemed to know what she was thinking.

"What are you staring at?" she demanded. She broke away and started rummaging in her locker.

"Nothing. Look, I'm sorry, Jessica. But it's not like my grandparents are going to have a fiftieth anniversary every year."

"I know," she grumbled.

"So don't be mad."

She sniffed. "I'm not mad."

"Then don't be whatever you are," he said.

Jessica whirled around and waved a fist in his face. "Boy, you're really asking for it," she warned. A laugh bubbled up inside her as he caught her again in his arms. It was hard to stay mad at A.J. for long, even though she was still more than a little ticked off about the upcoming weekend. She tossed her sunny gold hair back over her shoulders and gave him a stern look. "You'll just have to make it up to me later," she said, her voice low.

A.J. chuckled. "It's a deal. Hey," he added

casually as he pulled a folded sheet of paper out of his pocket. "I almost forgot."

"What?" Jessica arched her eyebrows.

"Well, I stopped in at the office when I got to school, and—" He held out the paper so she could see it.

Jessica dropped her gaze to the creased sheet of paper and instantly took in the words. "You did it!" she shrieked, throwing her arms around him. "You won the essay contest! I knew you would!"

Laughing, A.J. untangled her arms from around his neck.

"You sneak!" Jessica cried, reading the announcement again. "I can't believe you waited so long to tell me. This means you'll be king of the Citizens' Day Ball, you know."

Jessica knew it also meant that, as his date, she would be the queen. That was something she didn't take casually at all. It had been a long time since she had really felt like the center of attention, and she deserved a night in the spotlight, she thought.

"Well," she said with a happy smile, "congratulations. I guess that makes up for you going away, huh?"

A.J. grinned mischievously. "I thought it might."

*   *   *

After dinner Elizabeth went up to her room to work on an article for *The Oracle* on the Big Sister program she and Enid Rollins had started. It had turned out to be even more successful than Elizabeth had expected, and she wanted to do a status report for the paper.

"Liz, have you seen my blue hoop earrings? I can't find them anywhere!" Jessica's voice drifted in through the bathroom that connected their bedrooms.

Elizabeth put down her pen for a moment and stretched her back. "Look in the bottom of the laundry hamper," she suggested with a grin. Jessica's room was always a disaster zone, and it took a miracle to find anything. "Or inside your sneakers, maybe?"

"Ha-ha."

"Just trying to help."

Jessica appeared in the doorway, looking peeved. "Some help you are," she grumbled. Her face suddenly turned pensive.

Elizabeth regarded her thoughtfully for a moment. "Is something bugging you?"

Her twin shrugged. "No." She walked into the room and flopped onto Elizabeth's bed and lay staring up at the ceiling for a minute. "Nothing exciting ever happens to me," she finally announced in a mournful voice.

There was nothing Elizabeth could say to that, because it was so totally untrue. Jessica created excitement wherever she went. But Elizabeth sensed there was something upsetting her sister, and she waited for Jessica to go on.

"Liz, do you ever get tired of doing the same old stuff with Jeffrey all the time?"

Startled, Elizabeth turned around completely in her chair to look at her twin. Something was definitely bothering Jessica. "No, why?"

"I don't know." Jessica let out a long sigh. "Every day A.J. and I go to the Dairi Burger after school. We talk on the phone every night. It's like we don't have anything to talk about sometimes—'cause I know exactly what he did all day and he knows exactly what I did all day."

A frown creased Elizabeth's forehead while she listened. "Maybe you need to have more time to yourself," she offered.

"Maybe. I don't know." Jessica rolled over onto her stomach and balled her fists under her chin. "And now he's going off to *Texas*," she continued in a voice full of indignation. "For four whole *days*. Over the *weekend*."

"Well, what's your point? First you're complaining because you guys spend too much time together, and now you're complaining because you get some time alone." Elizabeth shook her head. "Make up your mind, Jess."

Jessica pouted. "There's no way I'm going to Ken's party by myself," she muttered. "It's so unfair."

Elizabeth fiddled with her pen and glanced at Jessica. To her, it sounded as if Jessica was just feeling sorry for herself and was taking it out on A.J. With her temperamental twin, every little grievance got blown way out of proportion. Jessica was feeling gloomy about spending the weekend without a date, and it was bringing every other petty dissatisfaction out into the open. At times like this, Elizabeth knew, there was no remedy. Jessica would feel sorry for herself for as long as she wanted to, then snap out of it on her own.

"This is going to be the most boring weekend of my entire life," Jessica mumbled into the bedspread.

With an exaggerated sigh, Elizabeth pushed herself up from her chair and sat down next to her sister. "Jess, if you don't get up and get out of here, I'm going to tickle you till you beg for mercy."

Jessica let out a squawk and wriggled off the

12

bed. She sat on the floor, glaring at Elizabeth. "Great. I come in here for a little sisterly advice and sympathy, and what do I get? Threats."

"Listen, until A.J. leaves, why not just enjoy your time with him," Elizabeth suggested patiently. "Then you'll have a few days to yourself, and when he gets back, you'll really be glad to see him again."

"Maybe." Heaving another self-pitying sigh, Jessica stood up and plodded back to her room. "Maybe."

Elizabeth rolled her eyes as she sat back down at her desk. Jessica could be counted on to make a big production out of every little incident life handed her. And she would probably never change.

By Wednesday afternoon Jessica had sunk even deeper in gloom. She could barely manage a friendly conversation when A.J. drove her home after cheerleading practice.

"We're leaving in half an hour." A.J. stopped his car in front of her house and stared out through the windshield.

Jessica nodded.

"And we'll be back Sunday at one," he reminded her.

Jessica nodded again but didn't say anything.

"Look, I wish you wouldn't act so upset about this—"

"It's not an act," Jessica corrected. She jutted her chin stubbornly. "But don't worry about me. I can find something to do."

A.J. was silent for a moment. Then he sighed and put one arm around her shoulders. "Hey, I wish I weren't going, too. But it's only a few days. I'll miss you."

"Yeah. Me, too," she agreed, turning and pressing her face against his chest. She could feel his heart beat against her cheek.

"I'll call you as soon as I get back," he promised.

"OK."

"And we'll do something together on Sunday, all right?"

She nodded. "All right."

"So—I guess I have to leave now." A.J. pulled away and looked at her with a rueful expression in his eyes. "Bye."

Jessica wrapped her arms around him and kissed him. "Bye," she echoed in a pitiful voice. She pushed her door open and stood on the sidewalk. "Have a good trip."

"I will. You have a good weekend."

She managed a weak smile, but inside, she

knew it was going to be the worst, loneliest weekend of her life. As A.J. started the car and drove away, she turned and walked toward the house.

Four days, she told herself morosely. *What am I going to do?*

Two

At lunchtime on Friday, Jessica flopped into a chair at a cafeteria table where her best friends were sitting, then snapped open a can of diet soda. Lila Fowler, Cara Walker, and Amy Sutton were deep in conversation, and none of them looked up as she joined them.

Jessica slumped in her seat and glared at them, waiting to be noticed.

"So then Mr. Rizzo told him he could shape up and shut up or get a detention," Amy continued without pausing. She tucked a lock of her sandy blond hair behind one ear. "And then you know what *he* said?"

Cara and Lila leaned closer. "What?"

16

Jessica clenched her teeth. "Hi, Jess!" Her voice was bitter and sarcastic. "Nice to see you. Glad you could join us for lunch."

Her three friends looked at her with surprised expressions. "What's with you?" Lila demanded.

"Well, *excuse* me for wishing my friends were friendly to me," Jessica said huffily. "I guess that's just too much to ask."

Lila, Cara, and Amy exchanged meaningful looks. Since Wednesday they had been listening to Jessica whine and complain and feel sorry for herself, and their patience was wearing thin.

"Jess, you're being a real pain, you know that?" Cara said. "Just because your boyfriend is gone for a couple of days doesn't mean you've got a terminal disease. It's not like I throw a fit whenever I don't see Steve."

For months Cara had been dating Jessica's older brother, who was a freshman at the state university. Sometimes they didn't see each other for several weeks at a time.

"Yeah," Amy chimed in. "Lighten up, OK?"

"Maybe I just don't feel like lightening up, Amy." Jessica took a long drink of her soda, keeping her eyes lowered. Everyone seemed to be ganging up on her. No one cared that her boyfriend had been gone for two days and wouldn't be back for another two. There was no sympathy at all.

Lila breathed an audible sigh and jangled the gold bracelets on her arm. "So what are you doing this weekend?" she asked patiently.

"Nothing. I'm staying at home like an old hag."

A snort of laughter escaped from Cara, but she clamped one hand over her mouth. Her brown eyes danced with laughter. "Poor Jess," she crooned.

"You know . . ." Amy said to Lila in a speculative tone. She cast a quick, appraising glance at Jessica. "Before she started going out with A.J., she would've been cooking up some plan to snag some cute guy somewhere. And now look at her."

"Pathetic," Cara said dolefully.

"Pitiful," Amy agreed.

"Ah, the good old days." Lila sighed.

"Oh, give me a break," Jessica snapped. She folded her arms and sent a murderous look around the crowded cafeteria. She was in one of her foulest moods ever, and she didn't appreciate her friends having fun at her expense.

There was silence at the table for a minute. Finally Cara spoke up. "OK, Jess, here's the deal. We're going to the beach after school. Do you want to come, or do you want to go home and mope?"

Jessica shrugged and stared down at her soda. "I don't know."

"Come on," Lila coaxed. "Why don't you do something with us for a change? You're always with A.J. these days."

Nodding firmly, Amy said, "Right. We never see you by yourself anymore."

"Well . . ." Jessica thought she would let them insist a while longer before she agreed. She deserved a little extra attention at the moment.

Cara stood up and leaned across the table so her face was inches away from Jessica's. "Look, if you don't come, we'll do something so incredibly horrible and disgusting and embarrassing to you—"

"In front of everyone," Lila put in.

"And you'll never live it down," Amy finished.

Finally Jessica allowed herself a tiny smile. "Well, OK. I guess so. There's nothing else to do."

"Gee, thanks," Amy replied sarcastically. "That really makes us feel special."

Jessica rolled her eyes. "All right, all right. I really, *really* want to go to the beach with you guys after school. More than anything else in the whole universe. Nothing could keep me away."

"That's what I thought." Cara grinned at her

and sat down again. "So we'll meet after school and hit the beach."

The worn oriental rug that Lila used as a beach blanket was littered with magazines, tanning oil bottles, and candy wrappers. Lila was busy painting Amy's toenails, and Jessica sat and stared at the ocean while Cara read a quiz from *Cosmopolitan* out loud.

"Question three: Your man buys a new suit that you think should be burned and the ashes scattered. Do you: a) tell him he looks great; b) offer to help him shop for clothes the next time he goes; or c) scream and put a paper bag over your head?"

Lila shrieked with laughter.

"Yeow! Lila, you just slopped nail polish all over my foot!" Amy wailed.

"Sorry," Lila said in an unconvincing way. She dabbed at the peachy smear with a cotton swab. "So what's your answer, Jess?"

"I don't feel like taking some stupid test, OK? They're for dorks. Besides, school is supposed to be over," Jessica replied testily.

"Well, *sorry*," Cara answered. She peeled the foil off a stick of gum and popped it into her mouth. "Question four," she read, snapping the magazine for attention. "Your man has family obligations that take him out of town for several days. Do you: a) tell him you understand; b) offer to go with him; or c)—"

"Scream and put a paper bag over your head," Amy broke in, giggling.

Jessica made a disgusted noise and stood up. "I'm going swimming," she announced.

When no one said anything, she marched down to the breaking surf and let the water whirl around her ankles for a moment. Out farther, at least a dozen surfers were riding the waves.

Her friends' laughter drifted to her, and Jessica felt a surge of loneliness and betrayal. They were acting as if nothing were different, she thought. They weren't making the least effort to cheer her up, and they were all going to Ken Matthews's party later and didn't even care if she went or not.

I could disappear off the face of the earth, and they'd never know the difference.

Feeling completely rejected, she dove into an oncoming wave and swam a few quick strokes out. She cut through another wave and felt her hair dragging out behind her.

They'd really be sorry if I drowned, she added silently. *Then they'd wish they'd been nicer to me when they had the chance.*

21

When she was far enough out to tread water, Jessica turned and looked at the beach, letting the swells bob her up and down. Her three friends were still doing what they always did at the beach—talking, sunning, checking out the guys. They weren't even looking her way to see if the undertow was carrying her off to Hawaii. She could be drowning for all they knew.

Cara looked up and saw her watching them and lifted one hand to wave. With a sigh, Jessica swam back in to shore.

"We're going to the Dairi Burger," Cara told her. "Are you coming?"

Jessica wrapped her big red beach towel around her and huddled on one corner of the rug. "No. I don't feel like it." She shivered, staring at her sand-covered toes and waiting for her friends to cajole her into going. But they didn't even try.

"OK," Lila said breezily. "If you don't, you don't. But we're going anyway."

As Jessica watched in offended silence, Lila, Cara, and Amy began packing up their beach gear. Lila rolled the rug toward Jessica. "Excuse me."

Jessica scooted off into the sand. She couldn't believe her friends would leave without her. Of course, they had come in two cars, hers and

Lila's, so she wasn't really being abandoned. But she felt as though she had just been dumped out with the trash.

Finally they were ready. Cara slung her straw bag over one shoulder and smiled warmly.

Now she'll ask, Jessica told herself, relieved.

"See you later, Jess," Cara said. "Are you going to Ken's party tonight?"

Jessica gritted her teeth and turned to face the water again. "No."

"Good thing," Lila observed with a grimace. "The mood you're in, you'd spoil any party on earth."

Jessica gave her friend an evil look. "Thanks a lot, Lila."

"Don't mention it. Catch you later."

Amy gave a brief wave as they started off. "Bye, Jess."

When her friends had gone, Jessica sat slumped in the sand, feeling neglected and forgotten.

I'll just stay here by myself. A lot they care. I'll stay here till I'm so depressed I can't even drive home. I'll just sit here all night.

While a parade of dreary, disconsolate thoughts went through her mind, Jessica stared blankly at the Pacific. She was half aware of the setting sun, the emptying beach, and one lone surfer riding out the waves. The darkening sky seemed to match her mood. She was almost beginning to enjoy feeling like the most pitiful person in the world.

By the time her hair had completely dried, the light was fading. Jessica stirred herself, suddenly realizing she had been staring at the surfer for at least half an hour. Her rumbling stomach told her it was time to go home, so she started gathering her things.

As she stood up to shake the sand out of her towel, the surfer waded up onto the beach, his board under his arm.

"You're not leaving, are you?" he called out.

She looked at the boy, startled, as he came up to her. Up close he was cute, with dark curly hair and piercing green eyes. A flush of pleasure crept up her cheeks. "Excuse me?"

"I like having an audience," he went on. The look he gave her was warm with admiration. He dug the end of his surfboard into the sand. "So what's a gorgeous girl like you doing alone on the beach?"

Jessica felt a smile turn up the corners of her mouth. She always liked flattery. "Maybe I just came to check out the quality of the surfing," she said, giving the boy a challenging look.

The slow, seductive smile that spread across his face completely charmed her. "So what's the verdict? Do I pass?"

"Mmm. I guess. B-minus," Jessica said archly. She turned away to pick up her beach bag.

"What do I have to do to get an A?"

With her back to him, Jessica allowed herself a smile of pure enjoyment. Almost more than anything else, she loved flirting with boys. Especially good-looking, charming boys with surfboards.

"I'll have to think about it," she replied in a thoughtful tone.

He sat down on the sand, looking as though he were prepared to sit there for hours to talk to her. "Maybe if I took you to dinner you'd have a better idea," he suggested easily.

Jessica raised her eyebrows in astonishment. "Boy, you don't waste any time," she said.

He shrugged. "Why waste time? I knew ten minutes ago I wanted to ask you out. So why pretend?"

Fascinated, Jessica sat down and gave him a long, measuring look. As a cure for feeling neglected, what he was offering couldn't be beat. Having someone so obviously attracted to her was exhilarating after her lonely, self-pitying two days.

"Why pretend?" she echoed. "I guess you've got a point there."

He smiled again, and his vivid green eyes

seemed to see right inside her. "I know I do. What's your name?"

"Jessica."

"I'm Christopher," he said, extending one hand. When she took it, his clasp was warm and electric. "So will you have dinner with me, Jessica?"

She lowered her gaze to their hands. Christopher wasn't letting go until she said yes, she realized. She liked that. And really, she told herself, there was no reason not to say yes. She definitely deserved a little fun. It was better than staying home and watching TV.

She raised her eyes to meet his gaze. "Sure," she whispered, looking deep into his mesmerizing eyes. She noticed how seawater trickled down his muscular arms and how the last rays of the sun glinted off the droplets on his chest. No doubt about it, Christopher was attractive. "Just say where, and I'll meet you there in an hour."

Three

Jessica ran up the stairs to her room taking the steps two at a time, slammed the door, and threw her beach bag into a corner. As she stripped off her shorts and her bathing suit, she heard her sister in the bathroom that connected their rooms. She hesitated a moment, not really wanting to run into Elizabeth. The fewer questions asked about her Friday night plans, the better.

When she heard the bathroom door to Elizabeth's room shut, Jessica dashed in to turn on the shower. But while she was rinsing the salt from her hair, Elizabeth came back in again.

"Hi, Jess. I just need to get my watch."

"No problem," Jessica shouted over the noise of the shower.

She waited for her twin to leave without starting up a conversation. Even though she knew having dinner with a new friend was perfectly innocent, Jessica didn't want to get into a discussion about it with Elizabeth. Her sister would no doubt bring up ethical issues and problems, like whether this dinner was an actual date and if Jessica was planning to let A.J. know about it.

Of course the answer to that was definitely no. Without a doubt, A.J. would take it all wrong, and as far as Jessica was concerned, there was no point in telling him. There wasn't anything to hide, but why bring it up and risk hurting anyone's feelings. Especially after it was over. As sensitive as A.J. was, he was bound to misconstrue the entire situation.

The door shut again behind Elizabeth. For a moment Jessica stood still, letting the water beat down on her. A picture of A.J. entered her mind, and she felt a nagging twinge of uneasiness. But then his face was replaced by Christopher's, and a wave of nervous anticipation swept over her.

I'm not doing anything wrong, she told herself firmly. *There's no reason not to go have dinner with a guy. It doesn't mean anything. And I'm just ex-cited about it because . . . because I like going out to dinner at nice restaurants.*

Jessica chewed on her lower lip, trying to justify what she was doing. Her conscience wasn't completely satisfied. But her natural optimism quickly buoyed her, and she decided there was nothing to get worked up over.

She finished washing her hair and stepped out of the shower. It wasn't until she was dressed and concentrating on her makeup that Elizabeth came back in.

"Sorry to barge in on you again," Elizabeth said. "I keep forgetting stuff. Are you going out?" she asked, noticing Jessica in front of the mirror.

Jessica paused with her mascara brush half-way to her face. Her mind raced. "I met some-one on the beach," she said in a casual tone. She brought the mascara brush up and did her lashes carefully. "We're just getting a bite to eat together. Nothing special."

"Oh, yeah? What's her name? Does she live in Sweet Valley?"

"Chris," Jessica said evenly. It was just like Elizabeth to assume it was a girl, Jessica re-flected. So far so good. She hadn't even lied.

"I think Chris lives up in Pacific Shores,"

Jessica added. Pacific Shores was just up the coast a few miles, and was the first place that popped into her head. She hadn't asked where Christopher lived, and he hadn't mentioned it.

Elizabeth smiled and reached for a headband. As she slipped it on, she met Jessica's glance in the mirror. "I'm glad you're going out instead of moping around here," she said warmly. "Why don't you bring Chris to Ken's party if she wants to come?"

"Maybe. We'll see. Oh, and I have to take the Fiat." Jessica finished her lashes with one last, careful stroke, then turned to her sister with a wide, innocent smile. "Anyway, gotta go. See you later."

Minutes later she was in the convertible, driving up the coastal highway. It had been her suggestion to meet outside Sweet Valley—she didn't want to risk bumping into anyone she knew—but Christopher was the one who had picked the restaurant just north of town. With the radio playing and the tangy sea breeze rustling her hair, Jessica felt her spirits soar. She was going to have fun even without A.J. Lots of fun.

She was smiling with excitement when she finally pulled into the long curving drive of the Casa Sur. Behind her on the horizon there was still a thin line of orange below the huge dark blue sky. When she reached the top of the steep bluff, a parking attendant hurried out to meet her in front of the restaurant.

"I was afraid you wouldn't come." Christopher stepped out of the shadows by the door and walked toward her, a half-smile on his face.

Jessica felt her heart leap and was glad it was dark enough to make it hard to see. She didn't want him to realize how excited she was. "What made you think I might not show?" she asked nonchalantly, turning toward the door.

"I don't know. But I was hoping I was wrong."

"Well, you were. I'm here." Jessica stopped and looked at him. Now that they were inside, in the light, she could see his face clearly. He was just as cute as he had been on the beach, if not cuter. He was dressed casually in a white button-down shirt, open at the throat, faded jeans, and loafers.

"Let's see if they have any tables outside," he suggested, his eyes lingering on her. "I'm getting hungry."

For some reason his words sent a shiver up Jessica's spine. Everything he said sounded seductive and thrilling. Without speaking, she nodded and followed him inside. Soon they were seated at a table on the deck, surrounded by

31

flaming citronella torches. Their eyes caught and reflected the jumping torchlight. A magical glow seemed to envelop them.

"I want to know everything about you," Christopher began, once they had ordered dinner. His eyes gleamed in the shifting light as he leaned forward on his elbows. "Everything."

Jessica tipped her head to one side and took a sip of her water. A secretive smile curled her lips. "There isn't that much to tell you. I live in Sweet Valley, and I like the beach."

"I already knew that," Christopher said, grinning. "I want to know what makes you unique. Because I know you're one of a kind."

Thinking of Elizabeth, Jessica almost giggled. It was fun to meet someone who didn't already know she was half of a duo. And there was no reason he had to know she had an identical twin, anyway. She liked him thinking she was absolutely unique.

"OK—here's the Jessica Wakefield life story," she said in a teasing voice. She clasped her hands together like a child reciting a poem. "All-American family—one mother, one father, one brother, one sister, one dog. I'm a junior, I'm co-captain of the cheerleading squad, and I play tennis. I like to dance, go to movies, and eat. That about covers it, I'd say."

Christopher sat back, folded his arms, and regarded her thoughtfully. Then he grinned. "That's it, huh?"

Briefly the thought of A.J. flitted into her mind. One important detail she had left off her list was "one boyfriend." But since she would probably never see Christopher again, she didn't see any reason to tell him about A.J. It would just put an awkward barrier between them, and she wanted to enjoy the evening.

With a clear conscience she returned his smile. "That's it. Now, how about you? I told my sister you were from Pacific Shores, but I just made that up. So where do you live?"

"Oh, what difference does that make?" Christopher said with a laugh. "You know I bet you could do anything you wanted to," he continued after a pause. He gazed at her appreciatively. "I bet there isn't much you don't know how to do."

Jessica felt a ripple of excitement run through her. It was getting harder all the time to convince herself she was just having a simple insignificant dinner with Christopher—that it wasn't a date. The way he was looking at her meant *he* didn't think it was insignificant. And the undercurrent of secrecy that Jessica felt only made it all the more thrilling and intriguing. So far, the evening was like a fantasy.

When their food came, Jessica continued to talk about herself. But she didn't even make the smallest reference to A.J. Whenever she thought of him, Jessica swiftly forced him out of her mind. He wasn't there, so she didn't want to worry about him.

On the other hand, Christopher *was* there. And he was so obviously fascinated by her that she found herself drawn to him more and more. He kept asking questions about her, urging her to talk. Whenever she tried to ask him something about himself, he brushed her questions away with a self-mocking laugh.

"I'd rather hear about you," he insisted. His penetrating, compelling eyes rested on hers. "I've never met anyone like you."

Jessica blushed with pleasure. Everything Christopher said went straight to her head.

"Well, aren't you lucky you did," she said lightly, darting a flirtatious look at him.

He chuckled, and Jessica found herself staring at his mouth, wondering what it would be like to kiss him. When she realized what she was doing, she was momentarily flustered. She pushed her empty plate away.

"We could go for a walk on the beach," she suggested, not looking at him.

She couldn't believe what she was imagining about Christopher. And she couldn't believe that remembering A.J. didn't make her feel more guilty. She never wanted the night to end.

"Sounds good," he said.

Their waiter came, and Christopher asked for the bill. He paid immediately and then there was nothing else for them to wait for. Christopher caught Jessica's glance across the table and smiled. "Ready?"

"Mmm. Should we . . . ?" She let her question trail off as she stood up.

He read her mind perfectly. "Why don't you follow me in your car? We can park at the beach down at Sea Otter Point and walk there."

Jessica felt she was in a dream as she drove behind Christopher's Volkswagen convertible. Dinner had had a mysterious, reckless excitement about it, and she knew her evening with Christopher wasn't over yet. When he signaled for a right turn, she put the Fiat into low gear and pulled into the parking lot behind him.

Within minutes they were barefoot and walking silently through the wet sand at the water's edge. Jessica inhaled deeply and looked up at a blaze of stars. Even though they weren't touching, she could feel Christopher's presence with every nerve in her body. With every step, electricity seemed to run through her veins.

"Jessica . . ." Christopher halted and stopped her with one hand on her arm. She stared at him in the darkness. "I can't believe any of this is happening," he said in a wondering voice. "I feel like—like—"

Without even stopping to think, Jessica let him pull her into his arms. Then she was kissing him, her hands behind his neck. Tiny, silent waves lapped over their feet as they stood pressed together. Jessica couldn't think of anything but how much she liked kissing Christopher, how exciting and intoxicating being with him was.

Finally he stepped back a pace and held her at arm's length. "I have to see you again. You know that, don't you?"

She nodded, speechless and entranced.

"Tomorrow? Can I see you tomorrow?"

"Sure," she replied. Her voice was throaty and low. For a moment practicality asserted itself again, and she glanced unconsciously over her shoulder. "I'll meet you somewhere—not in Sweet Valley, though."

"Anywhere, I don't care. Just as long as we can spend the day together."

Silent, she turned and headed back to where they had parked their cars. When she reached the Fiat, she turned to him and kissed him again. She didn't care if what she was doing was wrong. It was what she wanted to do. "Why don't we meet in Pacific Shores?" she murmured against his shoulder. "There's a café on Main Street. I can be there by ten tomorrow morning."

Christopher hugged her so hard, she almost couldn't breathe. Then he released her and brushed her cheek with one hand. "I'll see you at ten," he said softly. After giving her one last look in the starlight, he climbed into his car and drove away.

Jessica stood leaning against the Fiat, her mind a blank. She didn't want to think about what she was doing. If she thought about it too much, she knew she wouldn't be able to go through with it.

Four

The next morning Jessica found a parking spot for the Fiat a few blocks from Main Street in Pacific Shores. It was a charming, romantic, old town, perfect for a rendezvous.

Her pulse accelerated as she headed for the café. Just thinking of Christopher brought color to her cheeks and made her eyes sparkle with excitement. Meeting him might be wrong, but she couldn't help it. It wasn't often that she felt so exhilarated.

"Jessica!" Christopher saw her first and ran toward her up the sidewalk. He caught her in his arms and kissed her.

"Hi," she uttered and stepped back to glance

around bashfully. She raised her eyes to his face, wondering if the night before had just been a dream. But she could see from the look in his eyes that it hadn't.

"I brought you something," he said, grinning. When she looked down, she saw he was holding out a single red rose. "A woman was selling them on the street," he explained as she took it. "Do you like it?"

Jessica nodded, secretly moved. It was such an incredibly romantic thing for him to do. She brought the rose to her face and inhaled the sweet, delicate aroma. "I love it."

"Stay here."

Before she realized what he was doing, Christopher had dashed across the street and down the block. Jessica stood rooted to the sidewalk, puzzled. A couple strolling arm in arm passed her and smiled, and Jessica felt herself blushing with happiness. She sniffed the rose again and waited.

Moments later she was astonished to see Christopher rounding the corner, his arms loaded with roses. Her mouth opened, but she couldn't speak.

"For you," he said triumphantly when he reached her side. He cradled the huge bouquet in her outstretched arms. "That was all she had."

"Christopher!" Jessica stared at the roses. They were a deep velvety red, glittering with water droplets. A heady fragrance surrounded her. The beginnings of a laugh started in her throat and bubbled up. She shook her head in amazement. "You're crazy, you know that?"

"I'm crazy about you," he countered. "Let's walk."

"Don't you wish you could live here?" Jessica asked as they ambled down Main Street. Tiny shops, boutiques, and art galleries under bright awnings lined the sidewalk. Behind wrought-iron gates, narrow alleys stretched back to sun-lit courtyards. "I love it here, I really do," she went on.

Christopher looked down at her with a warm glow in his eyes. "This can be our town. Our favorite place."

Jessica felt a twinge of guilt. How could she break the spell by telling Christopher she couldn't see him after the weekend was over? She knew it was unfair not to tell him about A.J., but it would only hurt him if he knew, she reasoned.

I don't want to spoil what we have right now, she told herself. *It's too perfect.*

She felt a confusing mix of emotions being with Christopher. Meeting him in secret made every ordinary thing seem more exciting, almost more real. And she had to admit he made her heart flip-flop every time he looked at her with his captivating, mysterious eyes. But she knew deep down that it was all just a fling, a thrilling, one-time romance. Once Sunday came and A.J. returned, it would all be over.

So I'll just have a good time while it lasts, she told herself.

They passed a souvenir shop, its window crammed with California mementos. Usually Jessica sneered at tourist junk, but everything seemed different that day. In one corner a trio of stuffed animals caught her eye.

"Look at the little seals!" she crooned. She pointed at the toy sea lion pups. "Aren't they cute?"

Christopher squeezed her hand. "Which one do you want?"

She smiled. "The one in the middle," she answered instantly. "The really tiny one with the enormous eyes."

"Come on."

He pulled her after him into the crowded shop. Jessica hugged her roses to her chest and waited while he plucked the tiny seal out of the window display and paid for it.

She watched him covertly. Everything Christopher did seemed spontaneous. In the back of her mind she realized she really didn't know anything about him, and it was almost impossible to believe she had only met him the day before. But none of it mattered. All that mattered was that they were together.

When they were out on the street again, watching a stream of pedestrians go by, Christopher let out a contented sigh.

"I bet everyone's jealous of me," he said.

Jessica arched her eyebrows. "Why?" she asked, even though she knew what he meant.

"You're the best-looking girl in town, and you're mine. If you were with someone else, I'd die of jealousy." Christopher's eyes were dark and serious, even though he was smiling.

"Well, I'm with *you*," she pointed out. "So there's nothing to worry about."

"I know." He gave her a long, appraising look and nodded. "I know."

A ripple of excitement tingled through Jessica as she met his steady gaze. It thrilled her to think Christopher would be jealous about her, after knowing her for only a day. But at the same time it made her feel guilty again, thinking about how she was lying to both him and A.J.

"Are you hungry?" she asked, turning away to break the intensity. "I'm starved."

"Then let's get something to eat. And we can go to the planetarium, too," he suggested. One of the main tourist attractions in Pacific Shores was the combination aquarium and planetarium.

She smiled angelically. "Sounds great."

For the next two hours, they ate, talked, walked, and laughed. Jessica found herself telling Christopher things she had never told anyone except Elizabeth, and he told her over and over that he had never known anyone like her. She was beginning to feel the same way about him.

It's like a dream, she told herself later when they were seated in the darkness of the planetarium. "Like a dream," she whispered.

"What?" Christopher turned to her attentively.

Blushing, Jessica realized she had spoken out loud. "I'm having a great time," she whispered.

Christopher's eyes were huge in the darkness. He leaned closer to her as the stars appeared overhead. "Me too." He kissed her softly. "I think you're fantastic."

Jessica sighed, suddenly wistful. Everything was so great, but so mixed up at the same time. Instead of trying to sort it all out, she decided to put it out of her mind and just have a good time.

After the planetarium show was over and

they stood blinking in the sunlight outside, Christopher looked at her intently, hopefully, "What about tomorrow?" he asked.

"Well . . ." Tomorrow. Sunday. A.J.

Frowning slightly, Jessica turned and walked to the railing around the otter pool. Below, a dozen sea otters cavorted in the water. But Jessica didn't really see them. After tomorrow it would all be over, and she knew that was the best way. She couldn't risk letting things get beyond her control.

"All right," she said finally, glancing up at him. She had to tell him about A.J., but she couldn't. Not yet. "But only until noon. I—I have to do something."

"Just until noon?" Christopher gave her a teasing smile. "What happens then, you turn into a pumpkin?"

Jessica giggled but tried to be firm. "Really, I have to go at noon. We can meet at—" She scanned her mind, weighing the choices. Before noon on a Sunday, most of her friends stayed indoors. It would be safe to meet somewhere in Sweet Valley. "At the beach."

"Where we met—yesterday?" Christopher shook his head in amazement. "I can't believe it was just yesterday."

"I know. Me, either." She looked at him for a

long moment, then smiled. "But anyway, there's still all the rest of today, right?"

Christopher nodded. "Right. Until noon tomorrow, you're all mine."

When Jessica got to the beach on Sunday morning, Christopher was already there. He was sitting on the sand, facing the ocean. She ran to him and plopped down beside him.

He turned with a surprised smile. "Hi."

"Hi, yourself," she shot back. She tucked her knees up and hugged her legs. It was overcast and chilly, a rare bad day in Sweet Valley. The beach was almost deserted except for a few joggers and beachcombers. Her chances of being seen with Christopher were almost nonexistent.

"I had a really good time yesterday," she told him. She looked out at the breaking waves, and a feeling of sadness came over her. "A really good time."

"You sound like it's all in the past." Christopher glanced at her when she didn't answer. "What's wrong?"

Jessica squirmed, avoiding his gaze. She wanted to put off telling him about A.J. for as long as possible. But maybe her time was up. Her weekend fling was over, and that was the way it had to be. Trickling sand through her fingers, she said, "I can't see you after today."

There was a long pause. The silence stretched out so long that Jessica finally had to look up. Christopher was staring at her, a look of intense hurt in his green eyes.

"Why?"

Jessica swallowed. "I—have to leave at twelve," she said lamely.

"That's not a reason."

"I know, but, see—" Frustrated and embarrassed, Jessica hunched her shoulders and let them drop. "I have a boyfriend," she mumbled.

"What?"

"I have a boyfriend," she repeated more clearly, raising her eyes to meet his gaze. The look on his face made her cringe. "I didn't mean to—I mean—he was away this weekend, and when you asked me to dinner, I just thought . . ."

Christopher shook his head, a small, rueful smile on his face. "I should have known," he said with a sigh. He picked up a pebble and tossed it down to the water's edge. "I knew a girl like you would have to have a boyfriend already. Hey, don't worry," he added when he noticed her stricken look. "I understand. Really."

Relief flooded through Jessica. It was so strong she had to close her eyes. "You do?" she whispered.

"Yeah, honest. I had a great weekend, and I'll never forget you," he said softly. "But I understand."

A gull cried overhead. The mournful, melancholy sound matched the gray, overcast day. But inside, Jessica felt as light as air. It had all turned out perfectly. No one would ever know, and she could keep her weekend with Christopher as a blissful, exciting memory. Her everyday life and her relationship with A.J. would never be at risk.

"I'll never forget you, either," she said with complete sincerity. She reached for his hand and twined her fingers through his. "Maybe someday . . ."

Christopher shook his head. "No. Let's just leave it this way," he said.

Jessica gave him a tender smile and nodded. "OK. I—I have to go now."

"OK. Bye."

He was looking at the surf again and didn't turn to watch her go. Jessica felt like a heroine in a tragic, dramatic love story. She lifted her chin and turned away. It was all over.

By one-thirty Jessica was a bundle of nerves. A.J. was due any minute, and she wasn't completely sure she could act normal. Memories of the weekend with Christopher kept popping into her mind, and she had to force herself to think of something else—think of A.J.

Out on the patio, she paced back and forth beside the swimming pool. Prince Albert, the Wakefields' Labrador retriever, watched her patiently from a patch of shade. It was clear from the expression in his big brown eyes that Jessica's agitated pacing puzzled him.

"Jessica! A.J.'s here!" Mrs. Wakefield called from the kitchen.

Jessica clenched her fists and relaxed them with an effort. Then she composed her face into a big welcome-home smile. The patio door slid open, and A.J. stepped outside.

"Hi!" she exclaimed and rushed toward him. She wrapped her arms around him in a hug. "How was the trip? What time did you get in?"

"Hi, Jess." A.J. laughed and hugged her back. "It was great. The—"

"I was so *bored* the whole time you were gone," she chattered on compulsively. She threw herself into a lounge chair and slipped her sunglasses on. "Ken gave his party on Friday, but I didn't go. Oh, and you know that basketball game on Thursday? We won that. So how was your grandparents' party?"

48

A.J. grinned and settled his long, lean frame into the chair next to hers. He tipped his head back to the sun and sighed. "It was great seeing all my cousins and aunts and uncles and everyone," he drawled sleepily. "I'm really bushed, though."

Jessica sat up and crossed her legs. She reached down for one of Prince Albert's tennis balls and threw it for him to catch. "I bet you were having such a good time you didn't even have a chance to miss me," she added.

"I did, though," A.J. said. He gave her a sweet smile. "I thought about you almost all the time, and I told everyone about you, too."

"Really? What did you say?"

He shrugged. "Just the highlights—pretty, funny, smart, exciting. You know." A.J. grinned again and looked at her. "I really did miss you."

"Well, so did I. Miss you," Jessica replied hastily.

Actually, she wasn't sure if she *had* missed him. From Wednesday night to Friday afternoon she had missed him, she decided. But then from Friday to Sunday morning she had wished time would stand still and he'd never come back. She had to admit that that didn't exactly qualify as missing him.

A.J. reached out and took one of Jessica's

hands in his. "It's great to be back," he said in a meaningful tone.

Jessica smiled but didn't answer. She knew he couldn't suspect a thing. The best thing for her to do was just keep her mouth shut and stay out of trouble.

In a way, it would be easy to do. No one knew about Christopher, so she wouldn't be discussing him with anyone. And on top of that, she realized with a shock, she knew almost nothing about Christopher—not even his last name or where he lived. She could have imagined the whole thing. It could all have been a dream, except for the toy sea lion on her bureau, and the one rose she had kept. It had nearly broken her heart to throw away the bouquet of roses, but there was no way she could explain *them* to her twin or her parents.

From now on, no more thinking about Christopher, she told herself. *It's all in the past.*

Five

On Monday afternoon Elizabeth stayed after school to work on *The Oracle*, and Jessica had cheerleading practice. Afterward, they rode home together in the Fiat.

"Are you going to the girls' basketball game tonight?" Elizabeth asked as she drove.

Jessica shrugged and looked out the window. "No. We're cheering at the playoffs, though," she said in a monotone.

"I was thinking about doing a story on Shelley for the paper," Elizabeth went on. Shelley Novak was the star center of the girls' varsity team. She was the chief reason the team was doing so well.

Jessica didn't answer. She was staring at the traffic, deep in thought. It was clear to Elizabeth that Jessica wasn't very interested in hearing about Shelley Novak.

"You know what I noticed when I was talking to A.J. today?" Elizabeth asked above the rush of the wind. She glanced at her twin, wanting to coax Jessica into a better mood.

Jessica pulled a strand of hair from the corner of her mouth. "What?"

"His accent." Elizabeth said with a laugh. "I think being in Texas made his southern drawl stronger. Don't you think so?"

"Oh. Maybe."

Elizabeth looked quickly at her sister again, but Jessica seemed preoccupied and far away. Shrugging, Elizabeth turned her attention back to the road. When she pulled the car up the driveway, though, she remembered something she wanted to ask.

"Enid and I thought we should have a meeting for all the big sisters," she said. They headed for the back door and walked into the kitchen. "Just to see how everyone's doing. What do you think?"

Elizabeth and Enid had recruited a number of girls from Sweet Valley High to join the Big

Sister program. So far it had been a success, and Elizabeth and Jessica each had a young motherless girl for a little sister.

Jessica opened the refrigerator and brought out a giant bottle of diet soda. "Sure. I don't care. Whatever."

"Is sometime this week too short notice?" Elizabeth prodded. "Or should we make it next week?"

Slumping at the table, Jessica poured a glass of soda and looked bored. "Whenever, Liz. Just don't make it on a cheerleading day."

"OK." Elizabeth sat across from her twin, feeling slightly hurt. Sometimes she wished Jessica would be a little more enthusiastic about the things she cared about.

Elizabeth tipped her head to one side and toyed with the salt shaker, darting speculative looks at her twin. Jessica had been out an awful lot over the weekend, but she had been very vague about where she'd gone. She had brushed aside Elizabeth's questions without really answering them. Not that it was any of her business, Elizabeth knew. It was just a little surprising, since Jessica had expected to mope around the house all weekend.

"Jess?"

"Huh?"

Just then he phone rang, and Jessica jumped out of her chair to get it.

"Hello?"

Suddenly Jessica's expression underwent a dramatic change. Within a split second Elizabeth saw everything from happiness and excitement to embarrassment and irritation pass across Jessica's face.

"I—no. You shouldn't have—"

There was a pause while Jessica listened. Elizabeth thought there was something very peculiar about the way her twin was reacting.

"I told you—" Jessica broke off and glanced over her shoulder at Elizabeth, then turned her back, lowering her voice. "No. I told you I can't—no."

The look Jessica had given her made Elizabeth feel a twinge of guilt at her eavesdropping. She stood up and went outside to get the mail. Whomever Jessica was talking to, she deserved her privacy.

When Elizabeth came back in with the mail, Jessica was sitting at the table again, her face stony. There was a tense silence.

"That was someone trying to sell magazine subscriptions," Jessica explained before Elizabeth even said anything. When Elizabeth gave her a look of mild surprise, Jessica added defensively, "They're so pushy, you know? I practically had to hang up on him—*her*."

While Elizabeth stood staring at her twin, Jessica abruptly pushed herself up from the table and ran from the kitchen. Elizabeth was taken aback. It was so unlike Jessica to act this way, nervous and embarrassed.

Elizabeth shook her head. She wondered what sort of trouble Jessica had gotten into now.

"I've decided for sure. I'm selling my car." A.J. glanced up from his homework and gave Jessica a hopeful look. "That doesn't bother you, does it?"

It was Tuesday night, and the two of them were sitting in the den at the Wakefields'. Jessica sat with her chin propped up on one hand while she doodled in her notebook with the other. She shrugged. "Are you getting another car?"

"Yes, but not till I decide what I want to get."

"Oh." Sighing, Jessica drew a long squiggly line with a curlicue at the end. She hated to admit it, but it was hard to get worked up about whether or not A.J. sold his car. And she didn't know why.

A.J. nodded. "So I figure I'll put one of those

For Sale signs in the car window. Someone will see it and call."

"Yeah."

"Is something wrong?" A.J. asked after a pause.

Jessica looked up and managed a smile. "No. Nothing's wrong."

With an effort, she dragged herself to the present. Her mind had been wandering aimlessly. "So. I can't wait for the Citizens' Day Ball," she said, giving him a bright smile. "You'll be king, and I'll be queen."

"Right." A.J. laughed and shook his head. "Personally, I think the whole thing is pretty dumb, but you really get into it, don't you?"

"Are you *kidding*?" Jessica rolled her eyes. "You just haven't lived here long enough to know. Everyone goes—the mayor, all the big shots—and it's even on TV, usually. Being queen of that dance is definitely a major deal, A.J."

And I'm not going to miss it for anything, she added silently. There was a lot of prestige that went with that honor, and she wanted to be the one who got it. The king and queen would get their own special table, get to start the first dance after the ceremonies, be the center of attention, have their pictures in the paper, not to mention being on the news. No, she didn't think it was dumb at all. And she was going to be right there when A.J. was crowned, so he could turn around and crown her.

That was one of the reasons why she couldn't let anyone know about Christopher. When he had called the day before, right in front of Elizabeth, Jessica had thought she would have a heart attack. But she had told him firmly not to call her again. It was over. Besides, she didn't want to risk losing her chance to be the star of the Citizens' Day Ball.

I mean, risk losing A.J., she corrected herself after a moment's hesitation.

"Do you have that book about Germany?"

A.J.'s voice interrupted her thoughts, and she looked at him guiltily. "It's—"

The phone rang. For a second Jessica felt a wild panic that it could be Christopher. But she had made it very clear she didn't want to hear from him again, so she put the possibility out of her mind.

Jumping up, she crossed the room and grabbed the phone. "Hello?"

"Jessica? It's me. Christopher."

Her heart made a frantic leap and began pounding in her ears. She could feel her face flushing, and she quickly turned her back on A.J. so he couldn't see her expression. With a sense of alarm, she realized her mind was a blank. She didn't know what to say.

"Uh—hi, Lila," she finally choked out.

"Lila?" Christopher's voice sounded confused. "This is Christopher."

Jessica gritted her teeth. "I know, Lila. But it's a really bad time right now, know what I mean?" With her back still turned to A.J., she closed her eyes in a silent prayer.

Don't let this all turn into a disaster!

"I know you don't want to see me anymore, but I thought we could just talk, just be friends. There's nothing wrong with that, is there?"

"Well—I *can't* do that, Lila. I told you yesterday I couldn't—"

"Don't do this to me, please?" Christopher pleaded. "We had something really special. Why just throw it all away?"

Jessica swallowed hard and darted a nervous look over her shoulder at A.J. He smiled calmly at her, and in return she forced as natural a smile as she could muster. She turned back again and spoke into the telephone.

"That's just the way it has to be, OK? I *explained* to you on Sunday."

"I know. I know you have a boyfriend, but that doesn't matter— "

"It matters to me," Jessica said forcibly. She

58

turned to give A.J. another smile and tried to sound perfectly at ease and natural. "Nothing you can say will make me change my mind, Lila. Got it?"

There was silence at the other end of the line while Christopher digested her words. Finally she heard him sigh in resignation.

"OK. I understand."

"Good. I have to go. Bye."

Before Christopher could say anything else, Jessica slammed the phone down. She stared at it apprehensively for a second, almost afraid he would call back. But then she remembered A.J. She didn't know if he'd paid attention to her end of the conversation, but she was sure it must have sounded pretty strange.

Jessica took a moment to compose her expression. When she rejoined A.J., she was looking amused and irritated at the same time.

"What was all that about?" A.J. asked. His brown eyes were wide with surprise. "Poor Lila. You really laid into her."

"Oh, well, you know Lila," Jessica stalled. She picked up her pen and clicked it rapidly several times. "She, uh, wants me to—" She broke off, staring at A.J., her mind a blank. A.J.'s eyebrows lifted a fraction.

"She wants me to go shopping in L.A. with

her the weekend of the Samaritans' Club dance," Jessica explained in a rush. "I told her before there was no way I could miss it, and besides, I can't afford to go. Lila thinks everyone's as rich as she is. And she just gets so unreasonable when I say I don't want to, like it's something *personal*, which it isn't."

When Jessica paused to catch her breath, she had a suspicion she was babbling on and on like crazy. The look of surprise on A.J.'s face meant her explanation sounded a little bizarre.

Trying to appear completely calm and unconcerned, she finished up, "So I hope she finally gets the message into her head. She can be really stubborn sometimes."

A.J. shrugged and gave Jessica a lopsided smile. "You don't have to go to that dance just for me, Jess. I wouldn't mind."

But I would.

Jessica smiled indulgently at him while the thought went through her head. She wasn't planning on going to the dance just for A.J. She was going for herself, too. Of course, she was proud of him for winning the essay contest, and she thought he would make a great king. She could just picture him standing on stage, accepting the crown. A.J. really deserved all the attention and honor he would receive.

But, still, the fact that *she* would get to stand in the limelight next to him was what made it so critical. The Citizens' Day Ball was one of the most prestigious dances of the year, and *she* was going to be center stage!

But as they picked up their books to continue studying, a momentary fear flickered in Jessica's heart. What if Christopher didn't stop calling?

When Jessica got to her English class on Wednesday, the teacher, Roger Collins, handed her a note from the office.

"They have something for you," Mr. Collins explained. "A message maybe, or one of your books? I don't know."

Jessica frowned at the note, wondering what it could mean. All it said was to go to the administration office when she had a chance. That didn't sound particularly urgent, she decided. But it was still mysterious.

So when class was over, she headed downstairs. She could stop by the office on her way to the cafeteria for lunch. The halls were jammed and noisy, as usual, and she had to struggle to get through the crowd. She stepped through the administration office door with a feeling of relief and stood at the counter. At the far end, a bouquet of flowers wrapped in pink tissue paper gave off a faint perfume.

"And what can I do for you?" said one of the secretaries.

"I'm Jessica Wakefield. I was supposed to come to the office," she explained.

A huge smile broke over the secretary's face. "Well, lucky you. You have an admirer." She chuckled as she moved down the counter. She picked up the flowers and handed them over. "These came for you during third period."

Jessica took the bouquet in complete astonishment. As she parted the pink tissue paper to look at the flowers, a sick feeling settled in her stomach. She didn't need to look at the note nestled amid the baby's breath to know whom they were from.

I have to get rid of these, she thought frantically. She sent a rapid glance around the office, searching for a trash can. But the secretary was still beaming at her, so Jessica hurried out into the hall again.

And ran into A.J.

"Hey! There you are. I was looking—Hey, what are the flowers for?" A.J. did a double take when he noticed the lavish bouquet in her hands.

A fiery blush swept across Jessica's cheeks. Turning away, she began striding down the hall toward the cafeteria. She had to think fast.

"They're not for me," she said quickly. She gave him a frightened look and immediately dropped her gaze. The pace she had set was giving her a stitch in her side—she was practically running.

Her mind a whirl, she dodged into the crowded cafeteria. She was nearly frantic for some kind of explanation for A.J. One of the first people she saw was Cara, and Jessica swooped gratefully down on her friend.

"Look what Steve sent you!" she gushed, shoving the flowers into Cara's arms. She carefully palmed the card and stepped back. The note went into her pocket while she bounced into a seat next to her astonished friend.

"Isn't he romantic? My brother gets these ideas sometimes," she explained to A.J. "He asked me to bring Cara some flowers today. Isn't that a riot? Isn't he great?"

She turned her wide, desperate eyes to Cara, pleading wordlessly with her friend. Cara seemed to get the message.

"He's always doing things like this," Cara said carefully. She kept her eyes on Jessica and gave her a slow nod. Then she smiled up at A.J. "You should get Jess flowers sometime."

"I'll remember that," he said easily, taking a seat. He leaned forward to smell the bouquet. "Nice. I wouldn't mind someone giving me flowers sometime, too," he added with a grin.

Jessica forced a weak giggle. "OK. You got it."

Soon her friends were deep in conversation, and Jessica felt herself begin to relax. By some miracle, disaster had been averted. Her amazing luck had held, she realized, but it had been too close for comfort this time. Much too close. And she would have to think up an explanation for Cara.

Six

The Dairi Burger was crammed to capacity on Friday afternoon. In a corner booth by a window, Jessica was squeezed in with A.J., Lila, Cara, Ken Matthews, Winston Egbert, and Aaron Dallas.

"I think I'm going to suffocate," Jessica cried. She was pressed into the corner. "And I lost one of my shoes. I think it's under you, Lila."

"Well, don't expect me to get it. I can't move, either," Lila replied dryly.

"Complain, complain." Winston sighed. He was the unofficial class clown. Sticking out his lower lip in an exaggerated pout, he added,

"We should be grateful for what we have, thankful that—"

"Yeah, yeah. Give us a break, Win," Ken cut in.

Winston sighed dramatically. "I don't get any respect."

"Hey, A.J." Aaron leaned forward across the table. "I saw you've got a For Sale sign on your car. What are you asking for it?"

Cara and Lila put their heads together, starting a conversation about a new music video. A.J. managed to prop his elbows up on the table to answer Aaron.

"Fifteen hundred. Are you interested?"

"It was just like the last one they did," Cara pointed out. "Same kind of stuff."

"Maybe," Aaron said to A.J. "I have to think about it."

Lila grimaced. "They're all pretty boring, if you ask me."

Ken and Winston scrambled out to get more food, and Jessica sat back, absently shaking the soda and ice cubes in her paper cup and staring out the window. The two conversations went on around her as she gazed vacantly out the window to the parking lot.

Someone was standing by A.J.'s car, with his back to Jessica. Someone with dark curly hair.

He turned around and looked right at her. It was Christopher.

"No!" Badly startled, Jessica lost her grip on her cup, and soda and ice cubes spilled all over the table and onto her lap. In the confusion, Jessica ducked her head to concentrate on cleaning off her jeans, while the others broke off to help mop up the mess with paper napkins.

After a few seconds of sheer panic, Jessica raised her eyes to peek out the window. There was no sign of Christopher. He had vanished.

"What is it with you lately?" Lila asked. She shuddered in distaste as she dropped a sodden napkin on the table. "You're so jumpy."

"What do you mean? I mean—no, I'm not," Jessica protested. She didn't dare look up at A.J., afraid he would see some sign of guilt in her eyes. "I just dropped my cup, *OK*?"

Lila raised her eyebrows. "*OK*."

"But why did you say 'no'?" A.J. gave her a puzzled look.

Jessica felt her face redden. "What?"

"You said 'no' just then."

"Oh. I—" Jessica scanned the room, her mind a blank. "I just—I dropped my cup, and it just came out," she explained falteringly. She looked quickly at A.J. and looked away. "You know?"

"Right. I just thought it was about something we were talking about."

She shook her head vehemently. "No. It wasn't."

While the conversation resumed, Jessica slumped down in the corner. Her glimpse of Christopher had been so lightning fast that she was tempted to blame her imagination. But she knew he really had been there. Jessica was pretty sure she had seen him the day before, as well. Now she was convinced Christopher was following her.

This is getting totally crazy, she wailed silently. *He's going to blow it for me.*

She was sure the look on Christopher's face had been accusing and angry, just like the sound of his voice on the phone the night before.

Jessica squelched a groan of pure frustration. No matter how many times she asked him— told him, *begged* him—not to call anymore, he kept calling. She was beginning to be afraid to answer the phone at all. He kept saying he just wanted to talk, but on Thursday night, his manner had taken a new turn.

"Were you just pretending to like me?" he had demanded indignantly. "Is that some kind of a kick for you? Does it give you a rush?"

She had hung up on him. There was nothing else she could do.

Suddenly itchy and uncomfortable, she nudged A.J. with her elbow. He turned to her with a question in his warm brown eyes. "Let's go, OK?" she asked.

A.J. gulped down the rest of his milk shake and nodded. "Sure. No problem." As they squirmed out of the booth, he added to the others, "See y'all at the beach tomorrow."

Jessica quickly headed for the door, not even looking to see if A.J. was following. She just wanted to get away from Christopher and the place where he had tracked her down.

On Saturday, Jessica spent a miserable afternoon at the beach, hunched over and hidden behind big sunglasses. Every surfer she saw made her heart skip a beat. She was terrified Christopher was going to show up and make a scene.

Why is he doing this to me? she wondered. *Why won't he just leave me alone?*

Frustrated and anxious, she stared out at the water, wishing for the day to be over. A.J. kept trying to entice her to go swimming, but she refused. It was bad enough being on the beach without standing up and calling attention to herself. If Christopher was there looking for her, she wanted to be as inconspicuous as possible.

And besides, every time A.J. said anything to her, she felt a flood of guilt. He was the nicest, most sincere, and smartest boy she had ever dated—and she had gone behind his back and cheated on him.

A dark-haired boy strode by with a surfboard, and Jessica felt herself freeze until she saw it wasn't Christopher.

I'm getting so paranoid, she told herself mournfully. *This is crazy.*

What worried her most was that Christopher would keep following and calling her until somehow A.J. found out. It would take some pretty fancy storytelling to explain her way out of this one, Jessica realized. In the past, she had always been able to spin some kind of believable story when necessary. But with A.J., she wasn't sure it would work.

And to be perfectly honest with herself, she knew she wouldn't blame him. If she found out that A.J. had spent the weekend with another girl behind her back, she would be livid. So if he learned about Christopher, who knew what might happen. And it would probably take a miracle to keep him from finding out.

"Hey, Jessica!"

She winced and turned around warily. She relaxed when she saw Jeffrey French walking toward her across the sand. She waved and gave Elizabeth's boyfriend a feeble smile.

"Isn't Liz with you?" he called.

Jessica nodded down the beach. "She's over with Enid and Olivia."

"Right. See you later."

Next to her, A.J. gave her a puzzled look. "Hey. Are you all right?"

"Wh-why?" she stammered, blushing.

He shrugged. "You seem kind of worried, that's all. Nervous."

"Oh . . ." Jessica searched her mind for a good excuse. "I have a French test next week— it's going to be a real killer."

"Pauvre enfant," A.J. said with a little smile. "Oh, hey, I was going to tell you—a guy called last night about my car. He's coming over tomorrow afternoon for a test drive, so either you can come over while I wait for him, or I can pick you up afterward."

Being at A.J.'s meant being away from her phone, Jessica realized quickly. Every time the phone rang it made her a nervous wreck, so any excuse to get away was welcome. She gave him a half-hearted smile. "I'll come over after lunch, OK?"

"Sure." A.J. sprang up from the sand in one lithe, athletic bound. "I'm going swimming. Want to come?" He held out one hand invitingly.

Jessica shook her head and hunched her shoulders a little more. "No, not really." She watched him stride confidently down to the water's edge and felt a stab of pain and confusion in her heart.

Why did I do it? she asked herself mournfully. *How could I have been so dumb?*

Sighing, she surveyed the beach once again, but Christopher was nowhere to be seen.

That night the phone rang while Jessica was getting dressed to go out to the movies with A.J. She stared at the extension by her bed, her jaw clenched. It rang and rang, then stopped. She held her breath.

"Jessica. For you!" Elizabeth's voice traveled through the bathroom. Both girls had telephones in their rooms because they got so many calls.

With a sinking feeling, Jessica tiptoed through the bathroom and poked her head around the door to her sister's room. "Who is it?"

Elizabeth was reading and didn't look up. "I don't know. A guy."

"A.J.?" Jessica asked in a hopeful tone.

"No, I don't think so," her twin replied absently. Elizabeth was intent on her book. "You'd better answer it."

Jessica glanced at the receiver of Elizabeth's phone as if it were a rattlesnake. "I'll get it in my room," she whispered. She went back through the bathroom and slowly picked up her own extension. Before she said anything, she called to Elizabeth, "OK, I've got it." She waited until she heard the click of her twin's extension. Then Jessica said fearfully, "Hello?"

"Jessica—please don't hang up on me again." Christopher's voice was strained and pleading.

She swallowed, near tears. "Why won't you leave me *alone*?"

"Because I love you, Jessica. Don't you realize that? I *have* to see you again."

"No." Jessica vehemently shook her head. "That's crazy. You aren't in love with—"

"Don't say that! I am. Don't you know that by now? I'd do anything for you, if you'd just give me the chance. Your boyfriend can't love you the way I do. And if he knows about us . . ."

An alarm triggered in Jessica's head. "What do you mean, if he knows?" she croaked.

73

"You told him about us, didn't you?" Christopher's tone changed suddenly as he answered his own question. "You didn't."

"No, and I'm not going to! I'm not telling him, and I'm not breaking up with him or cheating on him again, OK? Now just leave me alone."

There was a pause, and then Christopher laughed. It was a disturbing, menacing sound.

"You wouldn't—" Jessica choked.

All Jessica heard was the sound of the dial tone. This time he had hung up on her.

Jessica sat down hard on the edge of her bed. Her knees were shaking, and her knuckles were white from gripping the receiver so hard.

"This is crazy," she whispered, her eyes wide and staring.

The word *crazy* seemed to echo in her head. It was the word she had been using every time she thought about the way Christopher was hounding her. Crazy.

What if Christopher was insane? The question loomed like a black shadow in her imagination. Suddenly Jessica was afraid. She slammed the receiver down and stared at the phone in horror.

Fighting the trembling in her arms, Jessica walked stiff-legged back through the bathroom and stood in the doorway of Elizabeth's room.

She stared at her twin without a word, her mind reeling.

Finally Elizabeth looked up. "What's up, Jess?"

Jessica looked at her sister for a long moment, then looked away. Nervous, she moved to the bureau and began picking over Elizabeth's barrettes and hairbands and jewelry. More than anything else, she wanted to confide in her twin. Elizabeth was always so reasonable. Nothing like this would happen to her in a million years, but she could help if anyone could.

Jessica had gone to Elizabeth for help so many times in the past, and always her twin had bailed her out. But Jessica wondered if she shouldn't try to sort things out on her own for once. She also hesitated because she was afraid to see the look on Elizabeth's face when she told her about Christopher. Her two dates with this strange surfer didn't seem so casual and unimportant anymore. Jessica had certainly gotten more than she bargained for from her romantic fling.

"Jess?" Elizabeth's tone was concerned. "What's wrong?"

Jessica forced herself to turn around and give her sister a carefree smile. "I just wanted to borrow your pink sweater, and I was afraid you wouldn't let me, that's all."

"Sure," Elizabeth replied slowly. She sounded unconvinced. "Go ahead—it's in the closet."

With a sickly smile on her face, Jessica turned and started rummaging in Elizabeth's closet. She had gotten herself into this situation, she resolved, so it was up to her to get herself out.

But she was still terrified.

Seven

Jessica woke up with a headache on Sunday morning. For a few minutes she lay in bed with her eyes closed, feeling miserable and tired. All night long she had dreamed that she was being chased, and no matter how hard she struggled to get away, she couldn't escape. In the morning she felt as though she hadn't slept at all.

And it's all because of him, she complained to herself.

Jessica glanced at her clock. Her parents and Elizabeth were probably eating breakfast on the patio, as they often did on Sunday mornings. She could picture them happily munching on toast and reading the paper.

They don't even care if I'm being followed by some nutcase, she thought. *They don't know how horrible it feels.*

To be fair, she realized, they didn't know about Christopher. She wished at least Elizabeth would sense her trouble and take pity on her, though. But it wasn't going to happen.

She flung one arm over her face. "Boy, you make one little mistake, and you end up paying for it a zillion times," she grumbled.

Finally she got up and scowled at her window. It was a beautiful day. Pouting, she wondered why there was never a natural disaster when she needed one. Nothing short of a major earthquake could stop Christopher from ruining her life.

"Well, you're looking pretty *un*cheerful today," Mrs. Wakefield teased as Jessica shuffled outside. Alice Wakefield was youthful and pretty, with a playful sense of humor. Her sleek blond hair shone in the sunlight as she reached for her coffee.

Jessica stifled a yawn and eyed the breakfast table suspiciously. Then she slumped into a chair and sank her chin on her chest. She let out a long, pitiful sigh.

"Something wrong, Jess?" Mr. Wakefield asked mildly.

"No."

Silence descended again while the others pored over the newspaper. Jessica picked up a piece of toast and crumbled it into pieces. She sneaked a look at her sister, but Elizabeth didn't notice.

The more she thought about Christopher's last call, the more spooked Jessica became. She wanted to confide in Elizabeth about Christopher's creepy behavior, but something held her back. Not until things were completely desperate, she decided.

"If anyone calls me this morning, tell them I'm sleeping or dead or in South America or something," Jessica announced.

Her mother looked over the top of the paper. "Anyone? Does that include A.J. and Lila?"

"And Cara and Amy?" Elizabeth put in.

The only way to screen out Christopher's calls was to avoid all calls. Jessica ruffled her hair and avoided meeting anyone's eyes. "*Anyone.*"

Frowning, she pushed herself up from the table and wandered back upstairs. Until it was time to go to A.J.'s, she just wanted to be alone. After tossing and turning in her bed, she finally fell into a heavy sleep and didn't wake up until noon. Then she dressed, ate half a tuna sandwich, and drove to the Morgans' house.

A.J. was polishing the chrome on his car when she arrived. He smiled and snapped the rag sharply in the air. "Hey—just in time to help me do the windows."

"Hi," she muttered. She gave him a quick kiss and ripped off a section of paper towel. "I'll do them from the inside."

"That guy called again this morning," A.J. said, spritzing glass cleaner on the windshield. "He said he's in a real hurry, but he wants to take a test drive. He should be here soon." He handed the glass cleaner to Jessica.

She nodded as she polished the inside of the window, but she didn't answer. After a few minutes of silence, she noticed A.J. studying her.

"Jess? Something's bothering you," he said abruptly. She started to deny it, but he shook his head. "No, I can tell. You've been really edgy the last few days. What is it?"

Unexpectedly her throat tightened. There was no way Jessica could tell A.J. the truth. So she concentrated on wiping a streak on the window and shook her head.

"Maybe I'm coming down with something, I don't know," she said. "I'm sorry I'm being such a—"

The sound of a car pulling up interrupted

her. She looked up as the driver got out. She felt the blood drain from her face. It was Christopher. Jessica held back a gasp.

In a flash she realized he must have taken A.J.'s number off the For Sale sign when he had followed them to the Dairi Burger the other day. He certainly wasn't there because he was interested in A.J.'s car. He was there because of her.

Jessica was paralyzed by shock and uncertainty, but seeing A.J. stride down the driveway to introduce himself to Christopher spurred her to action. She clambered out of the car and stood there, not knowing where to look. Christopher and A.J. were walking toward her, talking.

"This is Jessica." A.J. introduced her with a proud smile. He nodded at Christopher. "Jess, this is Christopher. He's come to look at my car."

"Hi. Nice to meet you, Jessica." Christopher held out his hand.

Jessica was afraid she would start screaming, she was so tense. But Christopher was pretending he didn't know her—and she didn't know why. All she could do was act as normal as possible, or she would be the one to give their secret away.

She took Christopher's hand, and his grip was so hard she almost flinched. "Hi," she whispered. She refused to meet his eyes, and she yanked her hand back as soon as she could. Surreptitiously she wiped her hand on her pants. When she glanced up, Christopher was giving her a sardonic look. She quickly turned away.

"Anyway," A.J. began as he smiled and waved toward his Toyota, "it's six years old, but that doesn't really matter with Japanese cars, you know? It still runs great."

Christopher frowned thoughtfully and nodded, walking around the car and examining the body. "Was it ever dented or repainted or anything? It looks good."

"No. I bought it from a friend of my parents, and he takes 'defensive driving' seriously," A.J. replied with a laugh. "Not even a scratch. I put in new spark plugs two months ago, and I change the oil every two thousand miles."

Jessica twisted her hands together and tried to stay calm. Watching Christopher go through the motions of a perfectly ordinary, harmless conversation with A.J. was like a horrible nightmare.

"So, how about a test drive?" A.J. suggested. He dug the keys out of his pocket. "We can cruise around here or take it out on the highway."

Christopher smiled, then glanced at his watch. "Sure, but I have to go pretty soon, so we should make it fast."

"No problem. Let me—"

"A.J.!" Mrs. Morgan opened the front door and waved. "Another call about the car, honey!"

Jessica glanced nervously at A.J. She didn't want to be alone with Christopher.

"Can't you take a message, Mom?" A.J. gave Christopher an apologetic shrug.

Mrs. Morgan shook her head. "I'm in the middle of something, and this boy has some questions. Come on."

Torn, A.J. looked at Christopher. "Look, this will only take a second."

"I'm definitely interested, but I'm really late already," Christopher said doubtfully.

A.J.'s eyes brightened. "Look—Jessica can go with you. It's not like you're going to kidnap my girlfriend, right?" he said, chuckling.

Jessica stared at A.J., too stunned to say anything. She could feel Christopher's gaze boring into her.

"It's not a bad idea," Christopher drawled.

A.J. laughed again and tossed Christopher his keys as he headed for the house. Speechless, Jessica was left with Christopher.

"Let's go, OK?" he said in a casual voice.

She shook her head, her blue-green eyes wide with anxiety. "No."

"You want to explain to your *boyfriend* why not?" Christopher sneered and opened the car door.

All she could think of was what A.J. had said about kidnapping. What if Christopher was angry enough and disturbed enough to actually kidnap her? But how could she explain her fear to A.J. without giving the whole show away? Her heart pounding, she walked around the car and climbed in. Deep down, she was afraid she would regret it for the rest of her life.

Without another word Christopher started the car, backed down the driveway, and turned up the street. Once away from the house, he pressed down on the accelerator. The car raced through intersection after intersection, heading for the highway.

Jessica gripped the seat and stared at the speedometer. The needle hovered at sixty-five, and they were still on the town streets. Her mind was a blank. She didn't know what to do, and she couldn't speak. Christopher seemed a completely different person from the one she had met the weekend before. There was a frightening intensity to him now that gave her chills. The tires squealed as he wrenched the steering wheel to turn up the entrance ramp to the highway. Jessica felt tears well up in her eyes.

"What are you *doing*?" she whimpered.

He didn't say anything. They were speeding up the highway at seventy-five miles an hour. The Sunday afternoon traffic was light and scattered, but Christopher kept switching lanes for no reason. Jessica was rocked from side to side, her shoulder slamming into the door.

Without warning, Christopher turned into the exit lane and sped down the ramp, through a yellow light at the bottom, and into an empty shopping center parking lot. Suddenly he slammed on the brakes, and the car spun around and stalled.

Jessica's eyes were squeezed shut, and her body was rigid with fear. Even though they had stopped, she knew the ordeal had just begun.

"Have you told him about us yet?" Christopher said in a perfectly calm voice. He looked at her expectantly.

She shook her head slowly, staring back at him in horror. Her voice was ragged when she said, "No. And you won't, either."

"Then you have to go out with me again," he concluded.

She shook her head. "No way."

"Saturday. We can go somewhere together

Saturday night," he went on, ignoring her refusal.

"I'm busy that night," she insisted.

Saturday was the night of the Citizens' Day Ball. But even without previous plans, there was no way she would go out with Christopher again.

He stared at her, his green eyes seeming to burn. "Change your plans."

"No." Jessica made a sudden grab for the door handle, but Christopher was too fast for her. He lunged and locked the door. Jessica cringed, terrified.

"Don't do that. You could get hurt."

Giving her a threatening look, Christopher started the car again and floored the accelerator. When he spun the steering wheel, they were suddenly rocketing straight across the parking lot toward the building.

Jessica stared at the onrushing brick wall and felt a strangled cry tear out of her throat. "OK. All right, I will!"

The car stopped with a screech of brakes and tires, and Jessica caught herself from plunging forward. She was so frightened by that time, she couldn't even cry.

"I knew you'd change your mind," Christopher said. He beamed at her cheerfully. "I'll call you during the week, and we can make plans."

Still smiling, he put the car in gear and drove sedately back to the highway. For the entire ride back, he talked about all the fun, wonderful things they would do together, and Jessica stared blindly out the window.

I can't believe this is happening to me. This can't be real!

She had no intention whatsoever of actually going out with Christopher again. But she would have said anything to snap him out of that strange, frightening mood.

When they turned onto A.J.'s street, Jessica nearly cried with relief. As soon as the car stopped, she fumbled with the door handle and pushed with her shoulder. For one wild moment of panic she thought she was trapped. But A.J. was outside her door, pointing to the lock. Feeling foolish and embarrassed, she unlocked the door and climbed out.

A.J. looked at her curiously and then glanced at Christopher. It was clear he could see something was wrong. "How did it go?" A.J.'s voice held an edge of suspicion.

Christopher handed over the keys and smiled sheepishly. "I think I drove too fast," he explained. "The accelerator was softer than I'm used to. I guess Jessica was a little shook up. Sorry."

When she didn't say anything, A.J. shrugged. "Well . . . OK. So what do you think?"

"Let me think about it, and I'll get back to you, all right?" Christopher smiled again and strode back to his VW convertible. "Thanks a lot. I'll be in touch." With a wave, he climbed into his car and drove away.

Jessica and A.J. stood in the driveway after he was gone. Jessica felt too numb to speak. It was no longer merely a question of worrying that A.J. would find out. Christopher was dangerous, and she didn't know what to do about it.

"Is everything OK?" A.J. asked. He wore an expression of tender concern. "How fast *was* he going?"

With an effort, Jessica forced herself to smile. "Oh—it wasn't that bad. It's just that he stopped kind of suddenly a couple of times. I guess he was testing the brakes. That's all. Really," she added when A.J. looked unconvinced.

"You sure? I don't think I like that guy," he mused, frowning at the street.

Jessica clenched her jaw. "Me, either."

Eight

On Wednesday afternoon Elizabeth drove to the elementary school, on the other side of town from Sweet Valley High. She arrived just as the final bell rang, and hordes of small children started pouring out of the front door. Elizabeth waited for Kim Edgars to appear.

When Elizabeth and Enid had started up the Sweet Valley High chapter of the Big Sister program, Elizabeth had thought she would be too busy to take on a little sister of her own. But being involved in the matching-up process hadn't been enough for her. On paper, Kim had looked like the kind of little girl Elizabeth's heart would go out to. So she had volunteered.

Since then, Elizabeth had tried to do something with Kim at least once a week—either see a movie, go out for milk shakes, or play on the swings in the playground. Almost anything was all right to do, because the object of the program was just to be a friend to a lonely motherless child.

Trailing behind the crowd of yelling kids came a small dark-haired girl. The moment Elizabeth spotted her she waved enthusiastically. Kim's face lit up with excitement when she saw Elizabeth. She came running over.

"I didn't think you would really come," she confessed as she opened the car door.

Elizabeth felt her heart tighten. Kim had learned never to expect anything nice or good to come true for her. It was pitiful.

But she made herself give Kim a teasing smile. "Would I stand you up? Get on in here, you brat." Her twinkling eyes took all the sting out of her words, and the little girl ducked her head shyly.

"Do you want to go to the mall today?" Elizabeth asked as they headed downtown. "I need some books, and I thought we could pick out one for you. How's that?"

Kim nodded, her eyes shining. "OK."

"Good."

Sending her little sister a wink, Elizabeth signaled for a right turn. Soon they were in the parking lot of the sprawling Valley Mall, hunting for a space.

"There's one!" Kim said excitedly. She leaned forward and pointed.

Elizabeth made an exaggerated expression of relief and exhaustion, and the little girl giggled. Elizabeth pulled the Fiat into the space. Over in the next aisle, she saw a white Volkswagen convertible slow to a halt. The attractive, dark-haired boy in the driver's seat looked at her intently, almost as though he expected her to say something or wave to him. But Elizabeth ignored him. Flirtatious boys exasperated her.

"Come on," she said to Kim. Elizabeth swung her bag over her arm and led the way to the mall entrance. Kim walked close by her side and seemed a little overwhelmed. "Have you been here before?" Elizabeth asked.

Kim shook her head silently, and again Elizabeth almost winced. All of the things she and Jessica and their friends took for granted were magical experiences for the little girl.

"Liz?" Kim glanced over her shoulder as they passed through the doors. "Do you know that boy?"

Startled, Elizabeth looked back and saw the

boy from the parking lot just behind them. She faced forward again and took the little girl's hand. "No."

"Is he following you?"

"Of course not! He's just coming into the mall like we are, silly," Elizabeth teased.

Not wanting Kim to be worried, Elizabeth forced herself not to look back again as she led the way to the bookstore.

In minutes they were poring over the selection of paperbacks in the children's section. From the look on Kim's face, it was obvious no one had ever offered to buy her a book before. Her solemn expression made it clear she was considering her choice with extreme care.

"I loved this one when I was your age," Elizabeth said. She pulled *Johnny Tremain* off the shelf and handed it to Kim. "It's about a boy in Boston at the beginning of the American Revolution," she explained. "It's really good."

"Is that the one you want me to get?" Kim's voice was soft and uncertain.

Elizabeth's eyes widened with alarm. "It's up to you, Kim. Honest. Pick anything you want. Anything." She could have kicked herself for making the little girl think she didn't have a choice. With an encouraging smile, she said, "Listen, I'm going to look at some of those books over in the adult section, OK? You pick out the book you want and meet me over by the cash register."

"OK, Liz," Kim whispered. Her eyes turned back to the children's books.

Elizabeth felt both relief and pity as she walked away. Of all the volunteer jobs she had ever had, she thought this one was the hardest, because there was so much in Kim's life that she wanted to make better but couldn't. There was only so much she could do to help the little girl, and Elizabeth knew she had to be satisfied with that. Deep in thought, she wandered among the book racks.

"Why do you keep avoiding me?"

The dark-haired boy from the parking lot stepped out in front of Elizabeth without warning. She jumped, startled and annoyed. If there was one thing she was not in the mood for, it was being nice to a pest. Besides, this was one of the most arrogant, obnoxious pickup lines she had ever heard. She turned her back on him.

"Please leave me alone," she mumbled. Her cheeks flaming, Elizabeth wove through the aisles and saw Kim waiting for her up ahead. Elizabeth already had her money in her hand when she joined the little girl, and she paid for their books and hurried out of the bookstore.

"I need to go to the ladies' room," she told Kim. "Why don't you come in with me?"

A hasty backward glance told her the boy was still watching her, and she angrily pushed open the swinging door of the rest room. Fortunately it was in the center of the mall, with doors at the far end leading to the other side. In a few short minutes Elizabeth was leading Kim through the opposite pair of doors and back to the parking lot.

"We have to cut this short today," she explained as they reached the car. "Sorry."

Kim rewarded her with a luminous, grateful smile. "That's OK. I had a good time."

"Me, too," Elizabeth replied warmly. She looked back toward the mall briefly before smiling at the little girl again.

After Elizabeth dropped Kim off, she headed home and spent the time before dinner practicing her recorder and doing homework. After dinner she wrote down some questions to ask Shelley Novak about the basketball playoffs for the school newspaper. Finally she treated herself to one of the books she had bought at the mall. She was just settling down to read when the phone rang by her bed. She cast a frustrated glance at it and waited, hoping Jessica would pick up in the other room. Eventually the ringing cut off in mid trill.

After a pause to make sure she wasn't about to be summoned, Elizabeth started to read. She was already several pages into her book when there was a timid knock on her door. Elizabeth glanced up, wondering if it had been a knock or her imagination. The knock came again, but not any louder.

"Come in," she called out.

The door opened a crack, and Jessica peeked in. "If you're busy, I can come back."

"No—come in. What's up?' Elizabeth looked at her twin and saw that Jessica's face was pale and strained. "Jess?"

Jessica took a few hesitant steps into the room, then hovered near the window, not speaking. From the way she was looking down at the floor, it was obvious she was deeply troubled. Elizabeth put her book down and crossed the room to her sister.

"Jess, what's *wrong*?" she begged. Elizabeth's voice caught when she saw the look of anxiety on her twin's face.

"I—uh—" Jessica swallowed and tried to speak. "Liz, I—"

Elizabeth took Jessica's arm and steered her

toward the bed. Firmly pushing her sister down, Elizabeth sat beside her and clasped her hand. "Jessica, whatever it is you've got to tell me. I can't stand to see you so upset!" When Jessica still couldn't speak, Elizabeth got a glimmer of a suspicion. "Who was on the phone just now?"

"Oh, Lizzie!" Jessica spoke in a pitiful wail. Her face crumpled as she burst into tears. "Liz! What am I going to *do*?"

Baffled, Elizabeth put her arms around her twin and waited for the storm to pass. "It's OK. Just tell me what it is, Jess. We can work it out, it's all right."

But for several minutes all Jessica could do was cry in Elizabeth's arms. Once in a while she choked out a few garbled words, but Elizabeth couldn't make any sense out of what she was saying.

Finally Jessica's sobs died down. She sniffed miserably into Elizabeth's shoulder. "I'm such a total jerk," she cried. "I'm the stupidest fool in the universe. I can't believe I did something so mean and—and sneaky!"

"What did you do now, Jess?"

"I—last weekend when I—" Jessica's eyes were brimming with tears and she couldn't meet Elizabeth's searching look. "Remember I told you

96

last Friday I was having dinner with someone I met on the beach?"

Elizabeth nodded but looked puzzled. She didn't have a clue what her sister was leading up to. "Right. That girl Chris."

"Well . . ." Squirming, Jessica said, "I never really said Chris was a girl—you just took it for granted. . . ." She faltered to a stop.

Elizabeth's eyebrows arched in disbelief. "You mean—Chris was a *guy*? You met a guy on the beach and went to dinner with him?" Jessica's mysterious disappearances from the weekend before came back to her in a rush. "And then you were with him all that Saturday, and Sunday, too, weren't you?"

"Yes," Jessica admitted in a tiny voice.

"And—A.J.?" Elizabeth was almost afraid to ask.

Jessica pursed her lips and met Elizabeth's eyes warily. "I didn't tell him. I knew he'd be really hurt!" she rushed on, seeing the look on Elizabeth's face. "I couldn't tell him."

"Jessica." The name came out in an exasperated sigh. Elizabeth shook her head. No matter how many times Jessica did something wrong, Elizabeth always hoped she would learn her lesson. But there was no way to change things once they were done. "Well. So why are you so upset? Did A.J. find out?"

Jessica jumped up from the bed and began pacing. "No. That's not it. But he might. Might? What am I talking about? He *will*," she corrected herself with bitter sarcasm.

Elizabeth was bewildered, but Jessica stormed on. "See, Christopher keeps calling me and telling me I *have* to go out with him again. And, Liz! He follows me wherever I go," she added with wide eyes. "And he acts so strange and creepy, and he says I *have* to go out with him this Saturday, or he'll tell A.J." The words tumbled out so fast, Jessica was breathless.

Elizabeth couldn't think of anything to say. She just stared silently at her twin.

"Lizzie!" Tears started streaming down Jessica's face again. "What am I going to do? If he tells A.J., that's it! A.J. will hate me forever—I know he will!" Overcome, Jessica slumped down at Elizabeth's desk and started sobbing all over again.

Elizabeth felt a turmoil of emotions. On the one hand, she was shocked that her twin had cheated on A.J. so casually. But on the other hand, if Christopher truly was unbalanced in some way, Jessica was being punished more than she deserved. And another sneaking suspicion occurred to her, too.

"Jess? What does he look like? Is he cute, with curly brown hair? And green eyes?"

Jessica sniffled and ran one hand across her tear-stained cheeks. "Yeah. How—did you know?"

"He must have thought I was you," Elizabeth mused. Looking up, she explained, "I was at the mall today, and a boy was following me around, trying to talk to me. It must have been Christopher."

"It must have been him," Jessica agreed. "He won't leave me alone! It was the biggest mistake of my entire life, Liz. And you know what else?"

Wide-eyed, Elizabeth listened while Jessica told her about the scene in A.J.'s car, when Christopher threatened to smash them both into the shopping center wall. In a ragged voice Jessica concluded, "Liz, what am I going to do?"

Elizabeth hunched forward with her elbows on her knees and tried to think. Jessica didn't need a lecture on honesty and fairness at this point. She needed serious help.

"Look," she began, thinking hard, "the only way to get rid of this power he has over you is to tell A.J. yourself. *Yes,*" she insisted when Jessica flinched. "You have to tell him, Jess. Even if Christopher wasn't blackmailing you, you have to tell A.J. What you did to him just wasn't right. You know it, too."

Jessica nodded meekly, but the look she gave Elizabeth was pure despair. "I know, but I feel so bad, Liz. It'll really hurt his feelings."

"I know," Elizabeth went on more gently. "But Christopher is blackmailing you. You can't let him keep doing it. He can't force you to like him or go out with him. Or else when will he stop?"

"But if I tell A.J., he'll break up with me," Jessica whispered, looking down at the floor. "And I don't want to break up with him—I still like him. And I really want to be the queen of the dance, Liz. I want to so much."

Elizabeth let out a heavy sigh. "Oh, *Jess.*"

"I really do! I can't tell him before Saturday, Liz. I just can't."

"Is that the only thing that would matter?" Elizabeth asked. She looked sadly at her twin. "It's not breaking up with A.J. that matters as much as not being the star at the dance?"

A fiery blush swept across Jessica's cheeks. "That's—that's not what I meant," she faltered. She twisted a lock of hair between her fingers and sighed. "I'll tell him, Liz. But not until after the dance."

"It's your choice," Elizabeth said with a touch of disappointment in her voice. "But I think you're making an even bigger mistake."

"I'll make it work out, Liz. I promise," Jessica insisted.

Elizabeth tried to smile, to show Jessica she was on her side. It was another classic Jessica disaster. And, knowing her twin, the situation was probably going to get a whole lot worse.

Nine

"Isn't there any lettuce?" Elizabeth asked, poking her head into the refrigerator.

Jessica pulled open the silverware drawer and shrugged. "I don't know," she said. She glanced at the telephone and bit her lower lip. It was Friday evening, and Christopher had called every day that week—sometimes even twice a day. She knew it was only a matter of time before he called again.

She swallowed hard. The whole situation was getting too crazy to handle, and she just couldn't understand how she had gotten into it in the first place. She knew she and A.J. didn't always get along perfectly and that their relationship wasn't trouble-free. But she couldn't figure out how she could have let herself cheat on him. It was all too confusing. Between her worries about Christopher, her guilt over A.J., and her own mixed-up feelings, she thought she was going out of her mind.

"Oh, here it is. You know," Elizabeth continued, crossing to the counter with her arms full of salad fixings, "Steve hasn't been home in weeks. Have you noticed?"

As she scooped up a handful of forks and knives, Jessica sent her sister a distracted look. "What? Steve?"

"Right. I—"

Just then the phone rang. Both girls tensed and exchanged a worried look. Wincing, Jessica whispered, "It's him. I know it."

"Well, answer it," Elizabeth whispered back. She darted a nervous glance toward the living room, where their parents were talking. Elizabeth jerked her head toward the phone. "Go on."

Jessica squared her shoulders and picked up the receiver. "Hello?"

"Hi—Jessica?"

She swallowed and gave her twin an agonized look. "Hi, Christopher. What's up?"

Elizabeth's eyes grew wide with anxiety. She

103

stopped tearing lettuce and stood watching Jessica.

"I was thinking about what we're going to do tomorrow night," Christopher said. He sounded pleased and excited. "I can't wait to see you again."

"Oh, well—me, too," Jessica lied. Twisting the phone cord around one finger, she added, "I guess I changed my mind about us. I can't wait to see you."

"Really? That's great. I thought we could go somewhere for dinner, and then see a movie—or maybe go dancing. What do you want to do?"

Jessica resisted the urge to tell him just what she wanted to do—never see or hear from him again. But she couldn't. In order to stop him telling A.J. her secret, she had to keep him happy. But she had *no* intention of going out with him on Saturday night. At the last minute she would find a way to get out of their date. And until then, she had to go along with him.

"Dancing—I love dancing," she told him truthfully.

Christopher laughed. "All right. That's what we'll do. I'll—"

"Christopher, my mother's calling me," Jessica broke in. "I have to go now, OK?" Her eyes met Elizabeth's. "Call me tomorrow."

"I will. Bye."

Jessica hung up the phone with a sigh of relief. "Oh, man. This is nuts."

"You aren't really . . ." Elizabeth's voice trailed off.

"Are you kidding?" Jessica shook her head and started getting out plates and glasses. "I wouldn't go out with that creep in a million years. But I have to keep stalling him."

"You haven't told A.J. yet, have you?"

Jessica lifted her chin stubbornly. "No. I told you, I'll tell him after tomorrow night."

"But, Jess, the longer you wait, the worse it's going to be," Elizabeth pointed out. Her voice was strained. "Don't you see? When A.J. finds out you waited two weeks to tell him, he'll be even more hurt."

Privately Jessica had to agree. She knew what she was doing to A.J. was wrong. It was unfair, and she didn't need Elizabeth to point that out for her. But at the same time she kept seeing herself as queen of the Citizens' Day Ball. It was only a little more than twenty-four hours away. There was no way she was going to jeopardize her chance to be in the limelight.

Besides, she added to herself, telling A.J. before the dance would spoil the whole evening for him. It was a big honor for him to be the king of the dance, and it wouldn't be fair to ruin his moment of triumph. He wasn't the kind of boy who could simply shrug off something like that. It would hurt him deeply, Jessica realized. For that reason, as much as any other, she knew she couldn't tell him yet.

"Jess? Are you going to—"

From the other side of the door, Jessica heard footsteps approaching. "Shh," she hissed. "Mom's coming."

Elizabeth clamped her mouth shut but looked like she wanted to say something more. She turned away as Alice Wakefield entered the kitchen.

"I'll start the steaks," their mother announced. Arching her eyebrows, she regarded the unfinished salad and the plates and utensils still sitting on the counter. Because she worked full-time, Mrs. Wakefield had made it the twins' responsibility to help get dinner ready every day. But at the moment she didn't say anything.

Seeing her mother's expression, Jessica hurriedly picked up the plates and carried them into the dining room. She felt that her whole life was teetering on the brink of chaos and that one slipup would turn into a disaster. But she wasn't going to make a mistake. Tomorrow evening she was going to be accepting the crown from A.J., and she wasn't going to let anything or *anyone* get in her way.

"Stop pacing, Jess. You're making *me* nervous now." Elizabeth looked up from the book she was trying to read and glared at her sister.

Jessica flung her hands up and grimaced. "Well, I'm sorry, OK? It's hard to stay cool when a psycho's after you."

"He's not a psycho, Jess." Sighing, Elizabeth got up from her bed and went to the bathroom door. It was late Saturday afternoon, almost time to get ready for the big dance. "I'm taking a shower."

"Fine. Just fine. What am I supposed to say to him when he calls?" Jessica demanded. "Aren't you even going to stay here and give me some moral support?"

Elizabeth leaned her forehead against the doorframe. Sometimes Jessica's histrionics were too much to take. "I thought you had a story all figured out," she said wearily.

"I do," Jessica said. "But what if he doesn't call?"

"He will. He calls every day," Elizabeth pointed out. Jessica didn't answer, and Elizabeth went into the bathroom and turned on the shower. Through the rush of water she heard the telephone ring.

Right on time, she thought.

Leaning over, she turned the faucets off again and slipped back into her bedroom. Jessica was just picking up the phone.

"Hello?" Jessica's voice was strained and weak.

Elizabeth watched and listened, wondering how her twin was going to get out of her date with Christopher.

"Oh, Christopher," Jessica whispered. "No—my voice? Well—I—"

Jessica paused to listen, then nodded. "They think it could be strep throat," she croaked. "I have a fever, it hurts to swallow, and I feel sick to my stomach. . . . No—but we can still go. . . ."

What an actress, Elizabeth observed to herself and shook her head.

"Well, maybe you're—maybe you're right," Jessica said with an artistically placed gasp of pain. "I'm really sorry—you understand? Really?"

Jessica listened for a few more minutes and then threw Elizabeth a triumphant grin. Her voice was still feeble, though, when she said, "Well, thanks for calling. Maybe I'll feel better soon. Bye."

When she hung up the phone, Jessica raised two fingers in the air. "Yes!" she whooped, springing off the bed. She pranced toward Elizabeth and took a bow. "And the master does it again, thank you very much!"

"He believed you?"

"Why shouldn't he?" Jessica demanded. She stood in front of the mirror and piled her hair on top of her head. "Should I wear it like this tonight?"

Elizabeth shook her head. It didn't seem possible that Christopher would relent so easily. From everything Jessica had told her about him—his obsessiveness, his persistence—Elizabeth just couldn't believe it was all over and done with after a one-minute phone call.

"It seems strange he would let it go after he's called you so many times," she mused. She glanced anxiously at her twin. "Are you sure he believed you?"

Jessica whirled around. "Stop being so paranoid, Liz! Sure he did. Come on."

"OK," Elizabeth replied in a guarded tone. She knew she was being suspicious, but she couldn't help it. Jessica was as happy as could be, and looking forward to her big moment. She had already forgotten how nervous and frightened she had been. And that worried Elizabeth more than she let on.

"Listen, are you taking a shower or what?"

Jessica said excitedly. She was flinging shoes out of Elizabeth's closet over her shoulder. "Can I wear your blue sandals?"

Elizabeth nodded. "Sure." With a last doubtful glance at the telephone, she stepped back into the bathroom to take a shower.

Just forget about it, she told herself sternly. She made a serious effort to shake off her misgivings. *Stop worrying, and have a good time.*

When she was combing the tangles out of her wet hair a few minutes later, she could hear Jessica gabbing away on the telephone—to Lila, from the sound of the conversation. After a shriek of excited laughter, Jessica hung up and came into the bathroom.

"This is going to be so great," she said with a huge grin. "I can't *wait* for tonight."

Elizabeth met her sister's eyes in the mirror and managed a warm smile in return. Jessica had been looking forward to the dance for weeks, and Elizabeth realized she shouldn't try to put a damper on her twin's enthusiasm. She hugged her sister impulsively.

"Me either," she replied. "I'll be cheering the loudest."

Shortly after seven-thirty A.J. arrived to pick up Jessica, and as they were leaving, Jeffrey drove up to get Elizabeth. Within minutes they were heading up the driveway of the Sweet Valley Country Club, where the Citizens' Day Ball was always held. The clubhouse was ablaze with lights, and colorful Chinese lanterns lit the way from the parking lot. Already couples were dancing outside on the terrace.

Inside, the main room was decorated with red, white, and blue banners, and a dance band was playing on the podium at the far end. The crowd was a mixture of Sweet Valley High students and their parents, important citizens, and local celebrities. Elizabeth recognized the mayor; Lila Fowler's millionaire father; and talk-show host Jeremy Frank all within the first few moments, and she saw that the president of the Samaritans was shaking hands as he worked the crowd. Mr. and Mrs. Wakefield were already there, talking with Skye and Kurt Morrow. Camera flashes kept blazing like lightning. The whole place was dazzling, exciting blur of elegant dresses, tinkling punch glasses, and happy conversation.

"The coronation is around eight," Jessica whispered when Elizabeth found her. Her eyes were huge with excitement. "Get close to the front if you can."

Elizabeth grinned. "I will. Good luck."

"Luck?" Jessica looked amazed. "What do I need good luck for? It's in the bag."

Giggling, Elizabeth nodded. "You're right. See you later."

"Let's go outside and dance," Jeffrey suggested. He looked handsome and sophisticated in a blue blazer and tan pants. He took Elizabeth's arm and twirled her around once. "Under the stars. How does that sound?"

"Perfect," Elizabeth answered, smiling up into his face.

Hand in hand, they wove through the milling crowd and escaped onto the lantern-lit terrace. Elizabeth inhaled the cool night air, and a feeling of calm washed over her. It was a romantic, dreamy night. She smiled as Jeffrey took her in his arms and they began dancing. She rested her cheek against his shoulder and let the music carry her away.

"Excuse me."

She looked up, startled, as Jeffrey stopped. Beside her, a boy was cutting in.

Christopher.

At the same moment Elizabeth realized who he was, she knew he had mistaken her for Jessica. He had come to find her twin, and if he did, the truth would come out. Jessica would miss the moment of glory she had been anticipating for so long.

As Jeffrey shrugged and reluctantly walked

away, Elizabeth took Christopher's hand and tried to think.

"I guess you recovered," he said, his eyes shadowed. "You must be feeling a lot better."

"I—I am," Elizabeth faltered. The only way to stop Christopher from discovering her identity was to pretend to be Jessica, she realized. There had been other times when Elizabeth had impersonated her twin. But none of them had been so important.

She tipped her head to one side and gave him a coy, flirtatious smile. "You're not mad at me, are you?" she asked in Jessica's manner. "I just didn't want to miss this party."

Christopher looked down at her thoughtfully for a moment, and then he smiled. "I guess not," he said. The hand that gripped hers was tight and rigid, and he held her close to him in an ironlike embrace. "That's why I came, Jessica. I knew you'd be here."

"You're pretty smart," Elizabeth shot back. She swayed in his arms and gazed at him seductively while she pitched her voice low. "I'm glad you're here."

"Me, too."

Over her shoulder, Elizabeth saw Jeffrey looking at them impatiently. He took a step toward them, and Elizabeth knew he was going to cut in again. She caught his eye and shook her head minutely. Frowning, he hesitated but stopped. Fortunately he trusted her, and Elizabeth was confident he wouldn't cut in if he knew she didn't want him to. There would be time to explain later. But at the moment, she had to keep Christopher away from Jessica.

"Who's that guy you were with? You looked pretty friendly."

"Who, Jeffrey?" Elizabeth let out a silvery laugh and shook her head. "He's my best friend's boyfriend. That's all."

"That's good," Christopher drawled. "Remember I told you once I get pretty jealous."

Elizabeth kept her expression from betraying her inner feelings. She felt a strange mixture of nervousness and suspense. There was no telling what Christopher's next move would be.

"Do you know what time it is?" she asked him.

He twisted his wrist slightly to check his watch without letting go of her hand. "Almost eight," he replied. "Why?"

"No reason," Elizabeth said breezily. "Just wondering, that's all." If the coronation was scheduled for eight o'clock, she had only a few more minutes to go.

Christopher smiled mysteriously and tightened his arm around her. "Let's take a walk. There are too many people around, if you know what I mean."

"Sure," she whispered. Her heart gave an uncomfortable lurch, but she forced herself to smile. If Christopher wanted privacy for a little romance, she would have to find a way to deal with that. There were plenty of things she was willing to do for her sister, but kissing a stranger was not one of them.

As he turned to lead her down the steps, Elizabeth looked back at Jeffrey and tried to signal with her eyes. "It's OK," she mouthed. Jeffrey looked pained, but he nodded and headed back inside.

Elizabeth looked at the brightly lit building. Through the terrace windows she could see people dancing and laughing and talking. All Jessica needed was a few more minutes, Elizabeth told herself resignedly. That was all.

Then Christopher tugged her hand, and she let him pull her away into the darkness.

Ten

Jessica kept her feet moving automatically while her eyes swept the room. So much nervous excitement had built up inside her that if she hadn't been dancing with A.J., she would have been jumping up and down with anticipation. It wouldn't be much longer, she told herself happily. Then the spotlight would be shining directly on her. Her blue-green eyes shone like brilliant stars as she looked out over the crowd again.

"You look beautiful, you really do."

A.J.'s voice broke into her thoughts, and Jessica looked up in surprise. She had almost forgotten his role in her moment of triumph.

"Oh, thanks," she said offhandedly. She bit her lower lip and glanced around again. "When are they going to get started, anyway?"

A.J. grimaced. "I don't know—I have to read my essay, you know that? I hate getting up in front of a lot of people."

Privately Jessica thought there was nothing she liked more. But she just smiled and nodded. At that moment the man she had anxiously been keeping tabs on began to head for the podium.

"There goes Mr. McKormick," she whispered. She grabbed A.J.'s hand and stopped him.

Paul McKormick, president of the Samaritans and the evening's master of ceremonies, shook one last person's hand and climbed the steps to the microphone. The band broke off with a drumroll flourish, and the roomful of dancing couples settled down into an expectant hush.

"Hello, everybody," Mr. McKormick announced with a broad smile. He beamed and nodded. "And welcome to the Seventeenth Annual Citizens' Day Ball."

A round of enthusiastic applause interrupted him. He fussed self-consciously with his tie and grinned. Then he held his hands up for silence. "Thank you. Thank you all very much. The Samaritans are proud and honored to sponsor this event every year, and I personally am thrilled to see many folks here tonight that have been with us from the beginning."

Jessica suppressed a sigh of boredom. In her opinion speeches were a waste of time. Everyone always said the same thing over and over again. Rolling her eyes, she folded her arms and waited. She looked around at the crowd again as the host continued speaking.

"Of course, some of you are here for the first time," Mr. McKormick went on. "And I see we have a big group of young people this year, too. So I'd like to recap what the Samaritans are all about, because Citizens' Day means something very special to us."

"How long is this going to last?" Jessica whispered. She caught A.J.'s eyes and wrinkled her nose. He just grinned and winked.

"The Samaritans are professional men and women dedicated to the service of our community, promoting fairness in business and civic opportunities," McKormick went on. "And every year we honor those members of the community who we think are outstanding citizens." Applause greeted his last statement again.

Next to Jessica, A.J. pulled his folded essay out of his breast pocket and smoothed it out. It crackled slightly, and Jessica could see a faint blush of nervousnesss creep into A.J.'s cheeks. He noticed her looking at him and smiled shyly. Mr. McKormick went on and on, thanking members of the Samaritans and citing community service projects in the past year.

Come on, get on with it! Jessica wanted to scream. She clenched and unclenched her fists, then twisted a lock of her hair. She drew a deep breath letting it out through her nose. During another round of applause, somebody stepped up beside her and gently touched her arm.

"Jess?"

She turned, startled, to see Jeffrey. She raised her eyebrows a fraction, keeping half her attention on the podium so she wouldn't miss her cue.

"Have you seen Liz?" Jeffrey whispered. His voice was anxious.

Shaking her head, Jessica said, "I don't know where she is. She was dancing with you the last time I saw her."

"Right. But then this guy cut in, and she went somewhere with him. That was about five minutes ago. I thought she'd be back by now."

A cold shiver of uneasiness crawled up Jessica's spine. She stared apprehensively at Jeffrey. "What *guy*?" she whispered.

"I never saw him before, but she seemed to

119

know him," Jeffrey replied in a worried tone. He kept searching the crowd with his eyes. "He's about my height, dark hair—"

"Curly hair? And green eyes?"

Jeffrey turned back to her, a frown creasing his forehead. "Yeah. Who is he?"

"Oh, I—"

Feeling sick, Jessica bit her lip and shot a quick, nervous glance at A.J. He was reviewing his essay and didn't seem to be paying any attention to her and Jeffrey.

She swallowed hard, her mind racing. If Elizabeth had gone somewhere with Christopher, that meant Christopher had come looking for *her* and had found her twin instead. And it also meant Elizabeth was going along with the charade so that Jessica could still be crowned queen. But if Christopher was unbalanced, if he was actually *dangerous* . . .

"I had a quick look around the gardens," Jeffrey was saying. "But it's like they just disappeared."

Jessica's heart began pounding with a dull, steady beat. Her sister was out in the dark with a boy who was definitely obsessed, possibly a menace. And Jessica knew she had to find Elizabeth fast.

But if she could only wait a few more minutes, it would be time for her and A.J. to go up to the podium. Leaving before then would mean A.J. might find out about Christopher and not want her to be his queen. At the very least, she would be out of the room at the critical moment. Also, it would be the height of cruelty to tell A.J. the truth just when he was about to be honored on stage in front of a roomful of people. For his sake, she had to wait until later.

Liz will be OK, she told herself fervently. *Nothing can happen with so many people around.*

But at the same time her conscience asked her a nagging question: *What are you afraid could happen?*

"Just a few more minutes," she whispered, wincing as though in pain. She couldn't even look at Jeffrey. "I'll help you look."

As she locked her gaze on the podium again, Jessica gritted her teeth together. Maybe she was just letting her imagination get away with her, she speculated. After all, she knew she was always blowing things out of proportion. Christopher probably wasn't any real danger at all.

Liz will be OK, she repeated to herself.

"Don't you think we should get back to the dance?" Elizabeth forced her voice to sound normal, but inside, her nerves were stretched tight. The clubhouse was almost out of sight through the trees.

"No," Christopher replied. He held her firmly by the arm and was leading her past the clay tennis courts. In the distance, the rolling green golf course blackened into the night.

Without warning, he stopped, and Elizabeth stumbled slightly. His eyes searched hers in the light from the distant parking lot lamps.

"Jessica, when I met you, I knew we had to be together," he said, his voice low and hoarse. "I knew it."

"I knew it, too," Elizabeth said. She managed a cool, unruffled smile. Lowering her eyes, Elizabeth tried to pull her arm out of Christopher's viselike grip. But he held on tight. "Let's go back and dance on the patio, OK? That was really fun," she said.

Christopher turned away. "No."

Elizabeth's mind raced. She knew she had to keep talking, keep the situation under control. But she had no idea what was going to happen, what Christopher was planning. It was getting harder and harder to believe she hadn't made a huge mistake going off with him.

In the back of her mind, Elizabeth was reliving the fear and uncertainty that had taken over her world when she was kidnapped once before. For a few weeks, she had worked as a candy striper at the local hospital, and a disturbed young orderly had fallen in love with her. Unfortunately his way of showing how much he cared had been to knock her out in the hospital parking lot and hold her captive for several days in a primitive shack. It had been the worst experience of Elizabeth's sixteen years, one she didn't want to repeat now with Christopher.

But I had to keep him away from Jess, she said to herself. *There was nothing else I could do.*

"Could we at least sit down, then?" she ventured. Elizabeth knew that the farther away from the lights and the people they walked, the more at risk she was. She smiled bravely and moved closer to Christopher. "There's a bench over there."

He was silent for a long moment, and Elizabeth found herself wondering what he was thinking. Finally he nodded. "OK, Jessica. I really want to talk to you."

"I want to talk to you, too," Elizabeth echoed as they walked to the bench and sat down. He still kept his hand clasped around her arm.

"I've been thinking," he explained. "I know of a way for us to be together all the time."

A prickle of fear made the hairs on the back of Elizabeth's neck stand up. "What do you mean?"

"We don't have to go back there," he went on obliviously, nodding toward the distant lights and faint sound of applause. "We don't need them."

"But—" Elizabeth's throat closed up, and she had to swallow hard before she went on. "My parents are there, and they're probably wondering where I am."

Christopher's grip tightened. "No, they're not."

For a moment Elizabeth considered screaming. She certainly felt frightened enough to scream. But with the speeches and applause, who would hear her so far away? she asked herself with growing panic.

As a last, desperate effort she whispered, "I told A.J. I'd meet him by the door. He'll start looking for me in a minute."

"No, he won't!" Christopher yelled at her, his voice suddenly angry and harsh. He wrenched her arm and yanked her to her feet. "He won't!"

Elizabeth shook her head, speechless with fear. Christopher was staring at her, a furious intensity making his eyes enormous.

"Come on. We're leaving."

Her heart lurched. "No—I don't want to leave, Christopher. I—I'm not who you think I am!"

He laughed tonelessly and began dragging her toward the parking lot. "I know exactly who you are, Jessica."

"No!" Elizabeth planted her feet and tried to tear his fingers from her arm. She was nearly frantic. "Let go of me!"

There was a click, and the light of a distant overhead lamp gleamed along a metal blade. Christopher pressed the flat of the blade on Elizabeth's arm. Her heart seemed to stop.

For the space of several seconds, neither of them said a word. Then Christopher sighed heavily. "If you would only like me as much as I like you, I wouldn't have had to do this, you know."

He sounded so reasonable, so sane, that Elizabeth couldn't connect his voice with the cold metal against her skin. Behind her, the loudest round of applause so far burst out into the still evening air. She pressed her lips together, praying nothing unexpected would happen to trigger his irrational anger and praying at the same time that something would happen to set her free.

"What do you want me to do?" Her voice was a ragged whisper.

He jerked his head toward the parking lot. "We're leaving. Come on."

Breathing hard, Christopher strode across the lawn with Elizabeth stumbling behind him. His fingers gripped her arm like iron clamps, and Elizabeth plucked at them hopelessly. There was no way for her to break free, even without the threat of the knife.

Up ahead, the parking lot was illuminated by pools of light from tall lamps. Insects hovered around the bulbs, and a thin halo of mist glowed above the cars. Elizabeth had to bite back a yelp of pain as gravel wedged into her open-toed sandals.

"Christopher—please," she gasped, near tears. "Please don't do this. Whatever you want, let's talk about it. You're making a big mistake."

"I know what I'm doing," he insisted. He yanked her savagely and almost sent her crashing into a parked car. Suddenly his face softened, and he shook his head. "Jessica—you're making this harder than it should be. Just relax."

"I can't."

Elizabeth's teeth began to chatter. One moment Christopher was quiet and concerned, and the next moment he was angry and uncontrollable.

I have to get out of this, she thought wildly. *What can I do?*

She thought again about the crowds inside, the music, the applause, and the noise, and knew that even if no one heard her, she couldn't just go meekly with Christopher. She opened her mouth to scream.

"*Don't.*" Christopher pointed the knife at her again, his eyes narrowed suspiciously. "Just do what I say, Jessica. Everything will be OK."

Crushed, Elizabeth felt her shoulders sag. There had to be a way, but she didn't know what it was. They were still weaving through the parked cars, but ahead she recognized the Volkswagen convertible she had seen him driving at the mall. When they reached it, he took out his keys and opened the trunk.

"What are you doing?" she whispered.

He didn't answer but took out a short length of rope.

Elizabeth backed up a step. "No—"

Before she could turn and wrestle away, Christopher had grabbed her other hand and was tying her wrists together. Struggling wildly, Elizabeth kicked at his shins and tried to squirm out of his grip, but he was too strong. In moments she was trussed up tightly. Tears ran unchecked down her face.

"Don't make a sound, or you know what I'll do," he said in a menacing, quiet voice.

A numb, helpless fear had settled in Elizabeth's heart. She just stared at him mutely. She couldn't speak at all. The whole world had been compressed into one small space in time, and she had never felt more alone.

Christopher shifted the knife in his hand for a better grip and gazed at her thoughtfully. Then he pointed the knife at the trunk. "Get in."

Elizabeth's eyes widened still further. "No, please. I won't make any trou—"

He brought one hand up across her mouth, and the other around her waist to her tied hands. Overcome with panic, Elizabeth tried again to struggle away. No matter what she did, though, Christopher didn't lose his grip. He held on to her tied wrists and forced her back. The edge of the open trunk cut against the backs of her thighs until her knees buckled under her. As she collapsed, sobbing and still fighting, into the trunk of the car, Christopher swung her legs up and reached for the lid.

"No!" Elizabeth looked up through her scalding tears and saw the light disappearing. Then she let out a moan as darkness enveloped her.

Eleven

Jessica stood between Jeffrey and A.J., gnawing her lower lip and twisting her fingers together. Something was wrong, she could feel it. That Elizabeth had been gone so long with Christopher was making her feel sick inside. Mr. McKormick droned on and on without making any sense to her. A.J. was looking over his essay again for his signal.

Beside her, Jeffrey whispered, "Do you think I should go look for her?" His eyes were filled with worry.

"I don't know," Jessica replied. She glanced at A.J. and then at the podium. All around them, people were smiling expectantly and watching Mr. McKormick. No one knew the turmoil she felt inside.

"And now the moment you've all been waiting for," Mr. McKormick announced. He rubbed his hands together and beamed down at A.J. "This is the fifth year we've had our essay contest, and believe me, it gets harder and harder each year to pick one essay out of all the terrific entries we get."

A.J. smiled bashfully and fidgeted with his tie. "Wish me luck," he whispered to Jessica. She returned his smile mechanically.

"But we did pick a winner, and I'm proud to say the winning essay was written by a newcomer to Sweet Valley. I guess he settled in real fast," Mr. McKormick continued with a jovial smile. "So let's all give a big hand to A.J. Morgan. Come on up here, A.J.!"

Applause broke out, and Jessica watched A.J. mount to the microphone. He smiled, nodded, and waved to his parents. Jessica waited. Then, without warning, a suffocating fear overwhelmed her. She stood rooted to the spot, her heart churning wildly.

Liz! No!

Something terrible was happening to Elizabeth. There was no doubt in Jessica's heart or her mind. The inborn, unconscious connection to her identical twin went deeper than logic or common sense. Her sister was in danger, and that was all that mattered.

"What?" Jeffrey asked, clutching her arm. "What is it?"

Jessica stared at him blindly. She had to find Elizabeth before it was too late. With a strangled moan, she pushed past Jeffrey and plunged through the crowd.

Oblivious of the surprised looks and startled cries, Jessica fought her way to the terrace doors. She was frantic, desperate. Her entire being was focused on finding her sister.

"Liz!" she gasped, stumbling out onto the terrace. She looked right and left past the swinging paper lanterns and then sprinted off into the grass.

"Jessica! What is it? Wait!" Jeffrey was racing to catch up with her, and his voice held a note of panic. "Where is she?"

Jessica didn't have time to explain. Her feet were already soaked with dew, and she slipped on the grass. Panting, she stopped and looked around again. To her right, the golf course stretched off into the darkness. To her left was the parking lot. She winced, breathing hard.

"I'll look by the tennis courts," Jeffrey said. He veered off toward the right.

Still uncertain, Jessica clenched her fists and squeezed her eyes shut. *Where is Elizabeth?*

Her eyes snapped open, and she whirled around to face the parking lot. She didn't know *why* she was so sure all of a sudden. She only knew she was. Without hesitating any more, she raced toward the parking lot.

"Liz! Liz, where are you?" Her voice rang out in the stillness. Gravel crunched under her feet as she raced around the parked cars. Under the lights, neat rows of cars went off in each direction.

"Jeffrey! Jeffrey, this way!" she cried. She sent a frightened look in the direction of the tennis courts. She wasn't sure she could handle Christopher alone. In fact, she was terrified of ever seeing him again.

But she couldn't delay. She pushed herself away from the car she had been leaning on and dodged into the next clear aisle. Then she stopped. Off to the left, she had heard a sound.

She squinted into the dimness and tried to hear past her own ragged breathing. Then she heard it again: a car trying to start. Instantly she ran in the direction of the noise, and when she rounded the end of one long row, she saw Christopher's Volkswagen in a pool of light.

"No! Stop!"

Even as she screamed, the car's engine roared into life, and the car backed up on squealing tires.

"Jessica!" Jeffrey yelled from a distance.

Without stopping to think, Jessica ran directly for the moving car. Christopher's face was faintly visible through the windshield as he put the car in gear.

"Stop!" Jessica stumbled and practically fell against the car. She hammered her fists on the hood. "What are you doing? Where is she?"

Christopher's eyes grew wide with shock, and his mouth opened in a yell. By reflex, he leaned heavily on the horn, sending a strident blast into the night. Then he jammed on the brakes and jumped out of the car. "How did you get out?" he demanded, moving quickly to Jessica's side.

"Where is she? Where's my sister?" she sobbed. The sight of him made her want to scream, but she had to find her twin.

"Come on, I don't know how you got out. Get back inside."

Christopher made a lunge to grab her, but Jessica kicked him in the shin with all her strength. He gasped with pain. "Don't do that," he growled. He grabbed for her again, but Jessica jumped to one side.

"Jeffrey!" she screamed.

Footsteps pounded on the gravel, and Jeffrey launched himself out of the shadows at the other boy. Christopher hit the ground with a thud, and Jessica fought back a scream. The two boys began fighting and rolling on the ground. At the same moment she heard a banging, hammering noise from the back of Christopher's car.

"Liz!" In tears, Jessica ripped the keys from the car's ignition, ran to the trunk, and fumbled with the lock. "Lizzie!" she sobbed.

The frenzied banging increased while Jessica struggled to open the trunk. Suddenly the lid popped up, and Jessica saw her sister tied up inside.

"Liz!" she cried out in pain.

Elizabeth was trying to hold back tears. "Jessica! You found me!"

Crying with relief and fear and guilt, Jessica reached in to untie her sister's wrists. Her hands were shaking so hard, she almost couldn't do

134

it, but finally the knots came free. She helped Elizabeth clamber out of the trunk, and they threw their arms around each other.

"I knew you were in danger," Jessica choked, hugging her sister tight. "I could feel it. I felt like I couldn't breathe."

They broke apart and stared into each other's eyes. "We're so lucky," Jessica breathed. It seemed almost a miracle that she had found her twin.

Elizabeth managed a slight smile and nodded. Then they both became aware of the fight going on behind them. As Jessica and Elizabeth ran to help, Jeffrey emerged on top, pinning Christopher's arms up behind his back. Christopher went limp, all the fight suddenly drained from him.

The twins looked down at him with mingled horror and confusion. He stared at them bleakly, taking in for the first time the fact that there were two girls instead of one. He closed his eyes.

"Jessica." His voice was a whisper full of despair.

She shuddered and looked away.

"Are you all right, Liz?" Jeffrey croaked. He was breathing hard, his upper lip was cut, and his clothes were covered in dirt.

Elizabeth nodded. "Yes," she whispered.

"Who is this guy? What was he doing?" Jeffrey went on, angry and hurt and bewildered. "Why was he trying to take you—" His voice cracked, and he gripped Christopher's wrists.

"It's my fault," Jessica said, tears flowing again. "It's all my fault."

Elizabeth shook her head. "No, it's not, Jess. You didn't know he would try to do this!"

"But if I only would have told A.J. . . . ."

"Jess! Don't think about that." Elizabeth grabbed Jessica's arm. "Is it over yet? Did you get crowned?"

Jessica shook her head. "A.J. was just starting to read his essay when I left." She shrugged. "It's too late."

"No, it's not. Go on back," Elizabeth urged her.

"But, Lizzie!"

"Go on." Elizabeth glanced at Christopher and winced. "I only went with him so you could get what you wanted, Jess. Go on. There's still time."

Even though it seemed like an eternity, Jessica realized it had only been a few minutes since her blind dash from inside the country club. A.J. might not even have finished reading his essay yet. She sent a forlorn look back at the brightly lit building. It seemed impossibly far away and out of reach.

Her sister shoved her. "Go on." Elizabeth's voice was weary but firm. "Please."

Jessica looked searchingly into her sister's eyes. What she saw there made up her mind. "OK, Liz. I will."

Twelve

As Jessica ran back through the parking lot, she tried to put Christopher's defeated expression out of her mind. It was sad and confusing and scary, too. And she didn't want to dwell on what might have happened to Elizabeth if she hadn't found her in time. As her feet hit the path to the clubhouse, two security guards came toward her.

"Did you hear a scream?" one of them asked her.

She stopped and fought for breath. "Back there," she gasped, waving her hand. "My sister will tell you what happened."

"Right." They took off toward the parking lot.

Jessica watched them for a moment, then headed for the entrance. She only hoped she wasn't too late for what she had to do.

As she slipped inside she saw A.J. still at the microphone, reading his essay. She started squeezing her way to the front of the audience while he spoke.

"So in the years between now and 2000," he read, "the greatest advances we should work for should be social, not technological. We don't need a space-age, futuristic world, because the one we live in is so great. But we do need a new way of living together, of working and cooperating so that all the good things we have can never be lost or damaged. And I hope to be one of those people who bring those changes to Sweet Valley in the years to come."

There was a hushed silence as he finished, and then the crowd burst into loud, enthusiastic applause. Jessica looked up at him with shining eyes. But her heart was full. Hearing A.J.'s familiar voice filled her with a deep, aching sadness.

"Well, I think I speak for all of us when I say that was a wonderful, inspiring piece," Mr.

McKormick said, advancing to the microphone again. He held out his hand, and A.J. shook it. "Thank you very, very much."

The applause doubled, and A.J. lowered his head, blushing. He caught sight of Jessica at the front of the crowd, and his eyes lit up with relief. As Mr. McKormick launched into another speech, A.J. beckoned to Jessica.

Her eyes stinging, Jessica shook her head. A puzzled frown crossed A.J.'s face. He leaned down from the podium. "What's wrong?"

"I—" Jessica's throat closed up, and A.J.'s face became a blur through her tears.

"Jessica?"

"A.J., I-I don't—"

Abruptly A.J. stood up and looked at Mr. McKormick. The master of ceremonies smiled and nodded. "I just have a few more folks to thank, A.J. Don't get impatient, now."

A ripple of friendly laughter went through the crowd at McKormick's teasing words. But Jessica and A.J. were oblivious of it. A.J. jumped down from the podium and steered Jessica away by the elbow. When they reached a secluded doorway they stopped.

"What's wrong? Where did you go?" A.J. asked, searching her eyes.

Jessica pressed one hand against her chin to keep it from trembling. "I can't take the crown, A.J.," she whispered. "I don't deserve it."

"*What?*" A.J.'s voice was raw with shock. "Why not? What are you talking about?"

Fighting tears, Jessica shook her head. She knew how deeply hurt he would be if she told him about Christopher. She had to tell him soon, but not during his moment of glory. That would be too cruel. "I did something stupid and mean that made me realize I can't—"

"What do you mean? I don't understand!" A.J. looked distraught, his brown eyes wide.

For a moment Jessica was too overcome to say anything else. Just minutes earlier, in the parking lot, she had realized the truth. She never would have gone out with Christopher in the first place if her relationship with A.J. was solid. She knew she couldn't pretend any longer, but she couldn't believe how much it hurt to accept the truth. She thought her heart was splitting open when she looked at A.J.'s face.

"Are we breaking up?" he asked in a disbelieving whisper. The look in her eyes gave him the answer. An expression of pain crossed his face. "Why?"

"Because—A.J., I like you so much!" Jessica

choked. "But I can't handle a relationship with one boy! I just can't! I'm not ready for it."

In the beginning, Jessica had thought she would love A.J. forever. Her affection for him had been so deep, so overwhelming, so exciting. But for the past few weeks, she had cared more about what the relationship could give her than about A.J. And that was wrong. A.J. was too sensitive and caring a person for her to lie to him anymore.

"I just can't do it," she repeated. She wiped her tears and looked at him. "I'm really sorry, A.J. I didn't know I would feel this way."

A.J. looked as if he might cry, too, but he managed a painful smile. "I know. I guess—I always thought I was too boring for you. . . ."

"No! That's not it, honest," Jessica said in a pleading tone. She glanced over her shoulder. People were looking their way curiously from time to time while Mr. McKormick spoke. With an angry frown, Jessica turned her back on them.

"Honest," she went on. She put one hand on his arm. "You're the nicest, smartest, and most terrific boy I've ever known. But I'm just not ready to commit myself to one guy." Her voice was bitter and sad.

A.J. let out a long, drawn-out sigh. "I won't

try to argue. If you really want to break up, I understand."

"I do," she whispered, the tears starting up again. "I'm so sorry."

With a faint smile, A.J. asked, "Would you do something for me, though?"

"What?"

"Take the crown. Yes," he insisted when she started to protest. "It would mean a lot to me. There isn't anyone else I'd rather give it to tonight." When she still didn't answer, he lowered his voice, "Please. For what we had, Jessica. For the past."

Jessica knew her heart was breaking. No boy had ever meant so much to her before. And it was over. But she tried to be brave and cheerful for A.J.'s sake. "OK," she whispered, meeting his gaze. "For what we had."

A.J. kissed her softly, then took her hand. "Come on."

"And now it's time for the moment we've all been waiting for," Mr. McKormick finally announced. One of the Samaritans stepped forward with a shiny crown just as A.J. led Jessica back up to the podium. Grinning, Mr. McKormick took it and placed it on A.J.'s head. "Congratulations."

Jessica could see A.J. say "Thank you," but the applause drowned out the sound. Her heart was aching with a painful mixture of pride and affection, loneliness and regret.

"And now you have the honor of choosing the young lady who will share that crown with you," Mr. McKormick said into the microphone. With a sidelong smile at Jessica, he added, "I guess I don't have to ask which lucky girl it's going to be!"

A.J. held out his hand to Jessica. Trying not to cry, Jessica nodded.

"And your name is . . . ?"

Jessica thought she would burst into tears again if she opened her mouth. She kept her eyes on the floor, wishing for the ceremony to be over.

"Jessica Wakefield," A.J. supplied.

"Ladies and gentlemen"—Mr. McKormick beckoned to the woman holding the second, smaller crown—"A.J. has chosen his queen for the Citizens' Day Ball. Let's give her a big hand, everyone. Miss Jessica Wakefield."

To the sound of applause, A.J. took the crown and settled it carefully on Jessica's head. Then the lights went down, and a single spotlight isolated them from everyone else. Hand in hand, Jessica and A.J. stepped down from the podium and onto the dance floor. The music started up, and they began dancing in each other's arms.

"I'll never forget you," A.J. whispered, his lips near her ear.

Because everyone was watching, Jessica was still trying to keep from crying. But two tears slipped down her cheeks as she squeezed her eyes shut and pressed her face against his shoulder.

"I'll never forget you, either," she echoed. "Never."

At one in the morning Jessica and Elizabeth were sitting in their nightgowns on Elizabeth's bed. Jessica had her arms wrapped around her knees, an expression of deep melancholy on her face. They had not been able to talk earlier about the incident with Christopher because their parents were at the ball, and they didn't want to upset them. But as soon as they got home, they went over the evening's events.

"So then what happened?" Jessica asked with a sigh.

Elizabeth formed a mental picture of the scene in the parking lot. She told Jessica that the police had come, and she had had to answer a lot of questions. But Christopher had willingly answered everything they wanted to know, and surprised them all by asking for his own psychiatrist. It turned out he was a deeply troubled young man, undergoing therapy.

"Then they took him away," Elizabeth said. "I guess he'll get the help he needs."

"I can't believe I could be so dumb," Jessica muttered with deep self-reproach.

"Hey. It's not your fault. There was no way for you to know." Elizabeth yawned and gave her sister a tender smile. "And I'm really sorry about A.J. and you. Are you sure you don't want to talk about it?"

A painful expression flitted across Jessica's face as she shook her head. "No—not right now," she said softly. "Maybe some other time."

Elizabeth nodded in sympathy. She knew Jessica had cared something more for A.J. than for any other boy. It must have hurt so much for her to admit their relationship was over, and to be strong enough to refuse the crown.

But A.J. asked her to wear it anyway, Elizabeth mused. *He's really a great guy.*

"Well, I think I'm going to bed," Elizabeth announced. It had been a long, exhausting night.

She put one arm across Jessica's shoulders. "See you tomorrow, little sister."

Jessica looked up and smiled. "Right. See you tomorrow, big sister. I love you, you know that."

"I know," Elizabeth said, her eyes shining. "It goes double for me."

After school on Tuesday, Jessica, Cara, and Amy walked to the locker room together to change for cheerleading practice. Jessica was still feeling subdued from the weekend.

"So, you know the Varsity Club dance is coming up," Amy mentioned as they started changing. Her gray eyes rested on Jessica for a moment. "Do you think you're going to go?"

Jessica kicked off her flats and frowned. A week ago she would have said yes. But now that she and A.J. had broken up, she didn't know what her plans were. "'I don't know," she said softly. "Maybe."

"Well, I was just wondering . . ." Amy and Cara exchanged a look.

Brooding, Jessica changed into her cheerleading uniform and let her gaze roam around the locker room. The girls on the basketball team were changing for practice, too, and the room was noisy with laughter and the clanging of locker doors.

"Everyone in the jock crowd is going," Cara added. "And it's the same weekend as the last girls' basketball playoff game, so we'll have to go there to cheer and then get to the dance."

"It is?" Jessica looked up at her friends. Then she turned around to survey the basketball players. Off in the corner, Shelley Novak was tying her sneakers. "If they win it, Shelley will *have* to go, don't you think?"

Amy and Cara followed her look. Shelley Novak was the star basketball player, but she was also notoriously shy. Mostly it was because of her height. She towered above almost everyone else in the junior class. It was obvious that she felt self-conscious about being so tall, even though that was one of the reasons she was such a good basketball player. All of the cheerleaders had speculated at some time or another about whether Shelley would ever go out with a boy. As far as they knew, she had never had a date.

"Yeah," Amy mused. She lowered her voice, and a malicious glint lit her eyes. "But who'd ask her? She's such a beanpole."

Cara giggled, and Jessica nodded slowly. "Why

don't you ask her if she's going?" she suggested airily.

"No! You ask her," Amy scoffed.

Jessica shrugged. Maybe it was time to stop feeling sorry for herself and start to take an interest in things again. She straddled the bench and called across the locker room to Shelley.

"Shelley? Hi," she went on, smiling, when Shelley looked up. "Hey, are you going to the Varsity Club dance?" Behind her, Amy and Cara stifled shocked giggles.

A slow blush crept over Shelley's face. "I—I doubt it," she replied. Her eyes went past Jessica to Amy and Cara, then back to Jessica. She moved her shoulders self-consciously and lowered her head.

"Oh, just asking."

"You're terrible!" Amy hissed delightedly when Jessica turned back to them.

"What? I just asked her an innocent question, that's all," Jessica insisted. She stretched her arms over her head. Then she grinned devilishly. "But I bet she does go."

Amy snorted. "Come on. Give me a break. She never goes to any dances. And no boy is ever going to ask her—no guy likes to dance with a girl who's taller than he is."

"Some guys *like* tall girls," Jessica said. Her eyes danced with mischief. "I bet she goes."

Cara and Amy looked at each other and shook their heads solemnly. "OK," Amy said, trying to sound grave and regretful. "This is one bet you're going to lose."

*Will Shelley Novak have a date for the big dance? Find out in Sweet Valley High #55, **PERFECT SHOT**.*

MURDER AND MYSTERY STRIKES

America's favorite teen series
has a hot new line
of
Super Thrillers!

It's super excitement, super suspense, and super thrills as Jessica and Elizabeth Wakefield put on their detective caps in the new SWEET VALLEY HIGH SUPER THRILLERS! Follow these two sleuths as they witness a murder . . . find themselves running from the mob . . . and uncover the dark secrets of a mysterious woman. SWEET VALLEY HIGH SUPER THRILLERS are guaranteed to keep you on the edge of your seat!

YOU'LL WANT TO READ THEM ALL!

☐ #1: DOUBLE JEOPARDY   26905-4/$2.95
☐ #2: ON THE RUN   27230-6/$2.95
☐ #3: NO PLACE TO HIDE   27554-2/$2.95

EXCITING NEWS FOR ROMANCE READERS

Loveletters—the all new, hot-off-the-press Romance Newsletter. Now you can be the first to know:

What's Coming Up:
* Exciting offers
* New romance series on the way

What's Going Down:
* The latest gossip about the SWEET VALLEY HIGH gang
* Who's in love . . . and who's not
* What Loveletters fans are saying.

Who's New:
* Be on the inside track for upcoming titles

If you don't already receive Loveletters, fill out this coupon, mail it in, and you will receive Loveletters several times a year. Loveletters . . . you're going to love it!

Please send me my free copy of Loveletters

Name _____ Date of Birth _____

Address _____

City _____ State _____ Zip _____

To: LOVELETTERS
BANTAM BOOKS
PO BOX 1005
SOUTH HOLLAND, IL 60473

Special Offer
Buy a Bantam Book
for only 50¢.

Now you can order the exciting books you've been wanting to read straight from Bantam's latest catalog of hundreds of titles. *And* this special offer gives you the opportunity to purchase a Bantam book for only 50¢. Here's how:

By ordering any five books at the regular price per order, you can also choose any other single book listed (up to a $5.95 value) for only 50¢. Some restrictions do apply, so for further details send for Bantam's catalog of titles today.

Just send us your name and address and we'll send you Bantam Book's SHOP AT HOME CATALOG!